Dying
to
Tell
Me

By Sherryl Clark

Kane Miller
A DIVISION OF EDC PUBLISHING

First Edition 2011
Kane Miller, A Division of EDC Publishing

For information contact:
Kane Miller, A Division of EDC Publishing
PO Box 470663
Tulsa, OK 74147-0663
www.kanemiller.com
www.edcpub.com

Jacket Design: Kat Godard, DraDog

Library of Congress Control Number: 2010943480

Printed in the United States of America
1 2 3 4 5 6 7 8 9 10
ISBN: 978-1-61067-063-0

To Kristi

Chapter One

I didn't want to sit in the front seat of our car – that's where Mum always sat – but Dad was pleading.

"Please, Sasha," he said. His voice caught, and he cleared his throat. "We promised a new start."

His face was so creased with sadness that I couldn't say no. I forced my foot and then my leg into the car and slid onto the dusty blue seat, yanking at the seatbelt. My hatred for Mum burned through me all over again.

"Bye, house," Nicky said, waving out the back window at the familiar cottage we'd lived in all our lives. I refused to look back.

All the way to Manna Creek, I hunched down in the seat and listened to my iPod. Nicky sat in the back seat,

1

clutching his box of magic tricks, staring out the window. Every now and then he'd go, "Wow," and point, but it was only something dumb like a cow or a sheep. I hated how enthusiastic he was, and knew it was mean, but meanness seemed to have replaced blood in my veins.

The moving van followed us like a lame dog that was scared it'd get lost before we made it to our new house. New *old* house. I'd already seen a photo of it, and it was beyond renovation. It needed demolition.

"Manna Creek hasn't had a policeman for six months," Dad had told us. "This is a golden opportunity to put the dirty, nasty city behind us and make a new life." I'd blocked him out – I didn't want to leave the city. But I'd lost my vote when I'd gotten into trouble and ended up in the Children's Court. If moving to the back of nowhere and becoming a country cop would make Dad happy again, I'd have to give it a try. I owed him that.

"Here we are," Dad announced, trying to sound cheerful. "Looking good, kids." A big sign flashed past that said *Manna Creek.*

"Watch out!" I screeched, my feet digging into the floor.

Dad slammed on the brakes, and I banged against my seat-belt. Behind me, Nicky's box of magic tricks clattered all over the back seat. A mangy yellow and brown dog skidded and leaped sideways off the road, then ran into the long grass.

My heart skittered inside my chest. The acrid smell of burning rubber filled the car. "Did you hit it?" I asked, sitting up, searching for the dog. What if it was injured?

"No," Dad snapped. "Don't yell at me like that again. I saw it before you did." He loosened his grip on the steering wheel and accelerated again, checking his mirror for the moving van.

"Sorry," I mumbled. Out my window, I caught a glimpse of a skinny guy with long, greasy hair shaking his fist at us. The dog cringed against his legs.

Nicky leaned forward between the seats. "Is this it? This is all there is?" He pointed ahead, disappointment tingeing his voice. My eyes followed his grubby finger.

A single street lined with old-people shops, a pub painted dirty-brown, another pub that'd been turned into an antiques place with a big *Closed* sign in the window, and a small supermarket with the windows painted over. There was not a single person in sight. If we'd been in a Western movie, a tumbleweed would've rolled across in front of our car.

It was even worse than I had imagined. I groaned.

"What's the matter? Are you carsick?" asked Dad. He patted my arm. "We're nearly there." He turned left, drove a short distance down a narrow street and stopped. "Here we go."

I couldn't bear to look, hunching down again. I turned my music up louder, drowning Dad out, but he pulled the buds out of my ears.

"Sasha, stop being silly and get out. The movers want to know where to put our stuff."

I shoved the buds back in, then slowly dragged them out

again, one at a time. I was being a pain, but I couldn't help it. My life had turned into a huge, weird disaster area that I had no control over, and I spent every day feeling anxious and stressed out. And hating Mum. At this rate, I'd have an ulcer before I was fourteen.

I pushed at the car door and stepped out onto spongy green grass that squelched under my feet. An icy wind nipped at my ears and nose. The house in front of me was like the photo, only worse. At least in the photo the rose bushes had been blooming. Now they were bunches of thorny sticks. The curtains were bedraggled, the front steps tilted sideways, and paint peeled off the siding. My skin puckered at the thought of thick, grimy dust and corners filled with huge, hairy-legged spiders.

The front door opened, and a blonde woman strode out, her heavy work boots ker-lumping on the wooden porch. "Hello!" she cried. "The kettle's on. And I've had a few local girls here cleaning up for you."

Dad marched up the trail and shook her hand. "Senior Constable Dennis Miller. We really appreciate this, don't we, Sasha?" He turned to me and frowned, his eyebrows angling down.

"Yeah, great, thanks," I muttered. Had they sprayed for big, country-type bugs?

Nicky had finished picking up his stuff from the back of the car and joined me. His mouth gaped. "It looks like it's going to fall down any minute," he whispered loudly.

Dad frowned harder. "It'll be fine, Nick," he said. "A coat of paint and it'll look like new."

Nicky pushed past me and nudged the mailbox that was leaning forward on the end of its pole. It toppled over and crashed to the ground. "Oops."

"I'm Cass Sullivan," the woman said, ignoring the mailbox. "Come on in and have a cuppa. I've made a pound cake."

As I stepped up onto the porch, I saw the stained glass door panels and the light, airy hallway, and my gloom lifted a little. Everything was clean and smelled fresh, even the bathroom that we all had to use right away. The movers started carrying in our furniture and placing it where they could find a space, and Cass Sullivan helped us lug in boxes. The cup of tea had to wait.

The house was small, our bedrooms only big enough for our beds and one chest of drawers. The family room couldn't fit both of our armchairs, and we had to leave the door open to get the couch in. Dad kept smiling the whole time, saying how great it all was, until I was ready to scream.

After we'd filled every available space, the rest of our furniture had to be stored in the big shed in the back. "Here," Dad said to me, "take this key and unlock it, will you? And make sure our other boxes are put at the front, or we'll never get them unpacked later."

I opened the back door and discovered that our house backed onto the brick police station in the next street. Between the house and the station stood a large, corrugated iron shed, and over to one side, a falling-down stone building. Its roof was a rotten-wood skeleton and half of a wall was missing, with ivy and blackberries winding in through the gaping window holes. The moss clinging to the stones was like disgusting fridge mold.

As soon as I stepped onto the scraggly lawn, my stomach started churning, tightening up and twisting around, and I could taste something sour and sharp in my throat. My head spun, and my vision blurred, with red tinges at the edges. I thought I was going to throw up, and I took a couple of deep breaths, reaching back to steady myself on the porch rail.

What had I eaten at our last stop? A doughnut and a hot chocolate. Maybe the milk had been off. I took more deep breaths, one hand rubbing my stomach, and slowly the blurring went away. I straightened up and swallowed hard, trying to get rid of the foul taste.

"You all right, love?" One of the movers had come through the side gate, and he gazed at me, his face filled with concern.

"Yeah, just a bad stomach." I tried to smile, but my mouth felt stretched and tight at the same time. I held out the key. "Can you open the shed?"

"Sure." He unlocked the padlock and pulled the sliding door across; it made a piercing screech. The shed was empty, the floor made of rough concrete, and it smelled of oil and dust. The other man arrived, carrying a large carton. "Where do you want this?"

"At the front," I said, and followed him into the shed.

As soon as I stepped over the threshold, the sick feeling disappeared. *Bizarre.*

I helped the men sort out where to put everything and made sure the big box with my name on it was put inside the house. I needed my collection of stuffed toys and my patchwork quilt that Grandma had made me. They had to be put out on my bed as soon as possible; they created my haven, my safe place, my fortress against the world.

In less than an hour, the truck was unloaded and the men gone, Cass had thumped away home, leaving us the cake, and Dad had scratched his head at the mess of furniture and boxes and said, "I might just nip over to the station."

"What about us?" Nicky said.

"Normally, I'd say keep out of trouble," Dad said, grinning, "but around here, I doubt there is any trouble." He sounded happily confident, as if we'd moved to Wonderland among the good fairies.

"You told us that bad people can live anywhere," I said. "That means Manna Creek, too." Although judging by the desolate main street, the worst that could happen here was jaywalking.

"This is different," Dad said. "You'll see. We're all going to love it here." The last bit was said with a tinge of desperation. It crept into Dad's voice every time he thought he wasn't being a good dad. But he was fine. He tried hard, and we muddled along. Not like Mum, who just cut and ran. Coward.

After Dad had left to open his new police station and

check it out, I found the box with sheets and towels, and Nicky and I made up our beds, although I had to help him. "You're nearly eleven," I said. "Time you were able to make your own bed."

He shrugged. "Who cares? I just sleep in it and mess it up again."

When my animals and quilt were arranged the way I wanted, with my stuffed tiger and wolf on my pillow, I sliced a huge piece of pound cake; I was starving, and it was way past lunch. I expected the cake to taste dry and bland, but it was moist and spicy, and I devoured another piece.

"When's Dad coming back?" Nicky said, helping himself to cake. "He said he'd help me set up my computer and find out about the Internet here."

I peered out the kitchen window – I could see between the shed and the stone building, right in through the back window of the police station. There was Dad, sorting through a huge pile of papers, filing cabinet open and two pens stuck behind his ears. My eyes veered left to the decrepit stone building, and my heart bumped against my ribs. Dizziness buzzed in my head, and I turned away quickly. What was happening to me?

"Let's get out of here," I said. I didn't want to stay in the house another minute. "Go and check out this dumb town."

The sky was dark gray, and a wintry wind chased dead leaves along the road. We put on our warm padded jackets and walked up to the main street. I'd been angry for months

— at Mum, at my so-called friends, at the whole world. I'd let it energize me. But as I gazed down the dreary street, the sodden gray sky felt like a heavy cloak, and my shoulders sagged. Two cafes. No McDonald's. No music shop. The supermarket had a pile of empty cardboard boxes stacked in the front. Even the antiques place with *Art Gallery* painted across its awnings failed to lighten my depression.

Nicky skipped towards a corner shop that looked like something out of "The Man from Snowy River," with carved porch columns and tiny-paned windows. "Hey, it's a deli," he said. "That means good stuff to eat."

"You mean junk food," I said, but my mouth watered at the thought of a big, comforting bar of chocolate.

The shop door, covered in a mosaic of product stickers, made a loud *ping* as we entered. Inside was jam-packed with cold cases, racks for magazines and newspapers, two long counters with glass windows, and a warmer full of pies and sausage rolls. I breathed in a combination of fresh bread, coffee and a cloying sweetness.

The shop was empty, and I wondered if we should ping the bell again, then something behind the counter moved, and a woman stood up. I stared — I couldn't help it — she was as wide as she was tall, with long red hair in two braids and a hand-knitted sweater in about a hundred different colors. She never said a word, just stared back at me.

Nicky poked me in the ribs, and I jumped. "What?" I snapped.

9

"Look at the candy," he breathed, leaning down, his nose almost pressed against the glass. "There's more candy here than ... a candy factory."

Finally, the woman behind the counter smiled. "Biggest selection outside of Melbourne."

Nicky fished in his pockets and found a dollar coin. "Can I have ... um ... there's too many to choose from. I can't decide."

She laughed, a raspy cackle that was like claws down a screen door. Goose bumps jumped up along my arms. "Do what my little lad used to do – start at one end and work your way down. You've got plenty of time to try them all out." When I scowled at her, she added, "Well, you are the new cop's kids, aren't you?"

"Sure are," said Nicky.

"Maybe that'll be two kids in town I won't catch shoplifting then, eh?" She cackled again.

My scalp prickled, and my mouth tightened. I'd had enough of people who made assumptions about me and Nicky because of Dad. What did she know about me? Nothing, that's what. I edged away from the counter and pretended to be interested in the magazines. "Hurry up, Nicky," I muttered. "Or I'll go without you."

He chose gummy snakes and jelly babies, paid and followed me outside, the white paper bag squashed in his hand. "What's the matter with you? She was nice."

"No, she wasn't. She was rude." He offered me a jelly baby,

10

but I shook my head. "Let's go that way," I said, pointing to a sign that said *Bungaloo Falls Walking Trail.*

Nicky followed me along the street, chewing on a red snake, while I inspected each shop we passed. Crafts and souvenirs, bakery, butcher, charity shop, supermarket with painted-over windows, used books. The place was for old people; four of them were bunched up by the butcher's shop, gossiping. The only two kids in sight were about five years old. By the looks of the last shop, *Magical Moments*, Manna Creek also had hippies who wore beads and tie-dyed shirts. Ugh.

But it's a great place for Dad, I reminded myself.

At the end of the main street, a well-worn trail carried on and then forked. One way was the falls walking trail, the other stopped abruptly at a rock monument that said it was part of a historical trail. I wanted to see the waterfall, even if it was only a dribble. The trail was slick with recent rain, and a thick layer of leaves muffled our footsteps. The bush closed in around us, silent and dark.

In five minutes we were at the falls; the water rushed down the narrow creek and poured over a high stone weir, spilling into a large brown pool ringed by low hanging trees. "Cool," said Nicky. "I wonder if people swim here in the summer."

I spotted a rope hanging from a tree. "I think so. Now what?"

"Let's walk along the river a bit," he said.

"It's not big enough to be a river," I said, but he'd scooted off without me, and I jogged to catch up. "Stick to the trail."

"Yes, bossy." A few minutes later he stopped suddenly, and I bumped into him. He held up a hand. "Listen."

Thump, thump, thump. "Look!" he cried. On the other side of the creek, four large gray kangaroos jumped away through the bracken, their heads bobbing like stringed puppets. Nicky's voice went all squeaky with excitement. "Were they real?"

"'Course they were."

"Wow, I saw real kangaroos!" He bounced up and down, looking like a kangaroo himself, which made me laugh. "They look weird when they hop. Maybe we'll see some more." He kept going, faster now, following the trail down into a hollow and around some rocks.

As I scrambled to catch up with him, my foot slipped, and I fell, lurching sideways. I grabbed for something, anything, to stop my tumble, but my fingers scraped uselessly at the rocks beside the trail. Down I went, falling, then sliding on my back, swamp grass lashing my face. "Help!" I yelled, panic flashing through me, my hands clawing at the muddy earth. Then I hit a tree branch on the bank with a huge *thwack* that knocked the breath out of me; I catapulted over it and into the water. The last thing I remembered was my head cracking against a rock in the water, and an icy blanket sliding over me.

Chapter Two

"Sasha? Sasha? Can you hear me? She's still unconscious. Get me another blanket for her. She should've come around by now."

It was Dad, his voice sharp. Had I done something wrong again? I tried to say *Dad, I can hear you,* but it was as if my mouth was frozen. Tremors rippled through my body, and my head was a balloon of pain. My jeans stuck to me like frozen glue, and I shook uncontrollably. Gradually, I felt a small hand in mine, warm and damp, and I managed a tiny squeeze.

"Dad! She squeezed my hand. Truly, she did." That was Nicky.

"Sasha? Can you open your eyes, love?"

My lids felt like heavy iron shutters, but I forced them open just enough to see it was dusk, trees black against a dark blue sky. People with flashlights were standing around me, their faces all in shadow. What were they doing? Who were they chasing?

"Bill, we need to get her to the hospital," said a man beside me.

"Yes, all right. Now that she's conscious … yes, of course." Dad suddenly sounded at a loss, the sharpness gone. Usually he was totally in command of everything. A dozen hands lifted me onto a stretcher, and my head pounded like there was an elephant in cleats jumping on it.

"All right, let's get her up to the ambulance."

No. Don't you dare move me again. I tried to raise an arm to stop them, but it wouldn't obey me.

They lifted the stretcher, and the world jerked and swayed. Nausea swelled in my throat, and I had to swallow over and over to force it back down. The stretcher was carried up the trail, brushing past bracken that sprung back with a *whip-whip* sound. I smelled something earthy and thick and heard boots squelching through mud. The ambulance doors were open, the interior lights making it look like a little room. A gurney was waiting. As the hands lifted me across to it, my head was bumped, and pain bloomed like red algae.

Had I passed out? Suddenly, I was being wheeled down a corridor with square grids of light above me. I squinted sideways and saw a white uniform, someone's arms, intent on pushing. I sensed others around me, drifting past. Hospital. The pain was like a thick pencil now, jabbing into my brain, and this time I managed to say something. "Head hurts."

"Yes, dear. But we can't give you anything until the doctor's seen you."

Great. Maybe they could stop wheeling me over bumpy ground then. Why did a hospital have rocks on the floor? Finally the gurney stopped and they lifted me onto a bed using the blanket I was lying on. "How old is she?" a voice asked. "Small for her age."

"Not my fault," I wanted to say.

"Estimate her weight then," the voice continued. "Start a drip first. And some hot water bottles when we get her clothes off. She's been in the water."

What? I was going to be naked? Wait. Let me …

Jacket, jeans, sweatshirt, undies – peeled off like I was a skinny orange. The rush of freezing air sent shivers rippling through me again, but soon I was covered in thick, fluffy blankets with four hot water bottles along my body. The shivering slowed, and warmth like melting chocolate crept over me.

Another voice. "Sasha, I need you to open your eyes."

I tried so hard I thought my eyeballs were going to pop out, but I made it.

"Good."

Poke, poke. Light in my eyes. Stop. Fingers lifted my head, probing the bit where all the pain was centered. It flared again like a stoked fire. I tried to push the hand away. The lights were so bright. I screwed my eyes shut to block out the glare.

Flash of a man, long, greasy hair hanging around his face. Looking at me.

"X-rays, and we might need a scan, but hopefully not. She'll have to go to Melbourne for that. Definitely concussion."

The voices droned on around me. More rumbling along on the gurney, metal plates, someone adjusting my head very gently. I followed the quiet instructions, praying for it to be over, and when someone bathed the back of my head in warm water, I cried. A mixture of careful dabbing and soft cloth, but still the pain arced brightly. Another gurney trip, a lift into a bed, and finally, when I was ready to strangle the nearest nurse in desperation, I heard, "Yes, she can have painkillers now, but she'll have to be watched."

Oh, I was so grateful! I broke out in a sweat of anticipation. Please, now, as many as you can.

I lay in the bed, trapped by the tightly tucked-in covers, waiting, wishing, trying to breathe lightly. At last the painkillers started to work, and the pounding dulled to a faint thrum. I was safe and warm, and the bright lights had gone.

Like a brief photo frame in my brain, a mangy brown dog growled, hackles rising, one yellow eye watching me.

"Sasha? Are you awake?" Dad and Nicky were creeping into my room like cartoon burglars. Nicky whispered,

"Ssshh," and lifted his feet higher.

"Hi." I tried to turn my head, but that was a bad idea. Silver stars zinged behind my eyes.

Dad grabbed my hand. "Thank God you're OK. When I got to the creek …"

"I pulled you out," Nicky said. "Well, sort of. You're pretty heavy."

"Did you?" I said.

"He did. He's a little hero," Dad said, hugging Nicky with one arm. "When I got there, your feet were still in the water, but you were shivering like jelly in an earthquake."

"Yeah, that's how we knew you weren't dead," Nicky said.

"How –" My throat was paper-dry, and Dad held the cup while I sipped water through a straw. "How did you know where I was?"

"Nicky came and got me," Dad said. "Told me to call the ambulance, too."

"I ran so fast. Zoom. You were like this." He let his head fall to one side like a floppy doll. "And your eyes were sort of open, but not."

I shivered. He made me sound like a zombie.

"I don't think you were knocked out for long," Dad said. "You were trying to talk when I got there, then you drifted off again."

"Sorry," I said, guilt flickering. "I didn't mean …"

Dad rubbed my hand with his warm fingers. "Nothing to be sorry about. I'm just glad you're OK."

17

A nurse came in and said, "You need to say good night now. Come back in the morning."

Dad and Nicky left reluctantly, but I was exhausted by the effort of trying to listen and talk. I closed my eyes.

Another photo flashed in my brain. The man again, standing over me, greasy hair falling across his face.

I jerked, eyes springing open. I knew who that was. The man beside the road whose dog we'd nearly hit. Had he come along while Nicky was running for help? If so, he hadn't bothered to pull me out of the water, he'd just stared down at me.

That's if he really had been there.

Not again, please, not again. I was breathing so fast, I was nearly panting. Air rasped in and out; I jammed my top teeth down on my lower lip and bit hard. It didn't stop my brain clicking like a machine, winding backwards. It'd happened before. People I didn't know, seeing things happening to them. And seeing other people that I shouldn't be able to. Because they were about to die. It was a long time ago, and it gave me nonstop nightmares. But I'd beaten it. I'd forced the things away from me, blocked them as hard as I could, and they'd stopped.

No, the man must've been there. I knew who he was, real, alive. He wasn't dying. I'd been the one in danger. Dad said I wasn't unconscious the whole time. I must've come to and seen him, then passed out again. My breathing slowed. Yes, he must live in Manna Creek. And he'd walked off and left me.

The nurse came back with a plate of lukewarm soup and

some buttered bread. "Sorry, this is all we've got at this time of night."

I forced some of it down – it tasted like split pea out of a can, thick and salty. She turned on the TV, but the screen made zigzag patterns in front of my eyes, so I lay there and listened. She said she had to check on me every half hour, which meant leaving the side light on. I flopped my hand up and down. Whatever. I drifted off to sleep.

In the morning, they decided to let me out. I had a mild concussion, but as long as someone kept an eye on me, and I stayed in bed, I could go home.

To that horrible, rundown house. I didn't want to go there, but I didn't want to stay in the hospital either. I wanted to go back to our old house in Melbourne, with the garden in the back, and our swings, and my old playhouse, and my green bedroom with the mural on the wall that Mum had helped me paint. A rush of homesickness washed through me and then fell into the black hole that Mum had left behind.

Nicky rushed into my room, brandishing my favorite jeans and sweatshirt, and saved me. "Your other clothes are dirty," he said. Dad's smiling face behind him lifted my spirits like a helium balloon. I didn't need Mum. I had Dad and Nicky. That was a million times better.

Dad wheeled me out to the car in a wheelchair. "I can walk," I said. "I'm not that useless."

"Hospital rules," he said. "And you'll stick to them when you get home, too, young lady."

Uh-oh. "What does that mean?"

"Staying in bed for the rest of the day, for a start."

He held my arm while I climbed into the car, and I didn't push him away because my head began to spin again. "I guess I'm grounded," I said, as he pulled the seatbelt down for me.

"No. I told you – this is not the big city. What happened to you was just an accident. Next time you'll know not to run along slippery trails." He got in on his side and sat for a moment, tapping the steering wheel. "Did you see anyone else out there by the falls?"

"I'm not sure."

"What does that mean?"

"When Nicky went to find you, I might've seen someone. A guy with greasy hair. But I probably imagined him. I was pretty out of it."

He grunted and started the car. I sagged back in the seat, glad he wasn't going to interrogate me. At home, I crawled into my bed and snuggled under my quilt, surrounded by my stuffed animals that watched over me with friendly eyes. Nicky tucked my gray wolf and my tiger up next to me. "Want a cup of hot chocolate?" he asked.

"No, thanks." My head ached, the jabbing pencil back, piercing my skull. I felt sick, and the last thing I wanted was food. "I might have a nap."

"You shouldn't sleep too much," Dad said. "You have to watch it with a concussion."

"Half an hour, OK?" I said.

Finally they left me in peace, and I closed my eyes, trying to visualize the pencil writing gently on my head *the pain has gone, the pain has gone.* It didn't work. The doctor had said it would take a few days to settle down. I sighed. My brain was doing its usual trick of leaping around, thinking of a million things at once. I'd been in so much trouble in the city, sending Dad nuts, but I'd never been physically hurt. Here in Manna Creek, I'd ended up in the hospital on my first day. Way to go, Sasha.

I wanted sleep, to blot everything out, stop me thinking too much, but it stayed out of reach. I wondered why Dad had asked about the man at the falls – maybe he'd seen the guy himself. Or maybe I'd gotten mixed up. Why had I seen flashes of him in the hospital?

I steered away from him and his mangy dog. School. Less than two weeks until the holidays ended. I'd be starting mid-year, the new girl with the cop for a dad. I hugged my tiger closer. I could hear the kids talking already – *super spy, snitch, informer, don't trust her* – even though tattling would be the last thing I'd want to do. In the city, I'd ended up as the bad girl and made them all look like amateurs.

Poor Dad had to come and get me from the police station – twice. Once for shoplifting, once for joyriding. The second time I'd had to go to court, and that was freaky. My face burned at the memory. Everyone looked about ten feet tall, and they'd all glared at me like I was evil. Only the lawyer Dad had paid for was nice to me.

21

The pain in my head grew sharper, and red flashes flared under my eyelids. I wanted more painkillers, but I'd just had some.

Photo flash: An axe arced down. Whump! Whump! A man was chopping the head off an animal. Staring eyeball. Blood.

"Ahhh!" I shot upright in bed, gasping. What was that?

Nicky came running in, pale and wide-eyed. "Are you OK? You screamed."

"It's – it was – nothing. Pain. You know? It comes and goes, really bad sometimes." I tried to smile, but my mouth wobbled. "Sorry."

"Should I get Dad?"

"No, it's OK. Can you – maybe I should have that hot chocolate. Can you make me some toast?" That was it – I needed food.

"Sure thing!" He grinned and raced off to the kitchen.

I lowered myself gingerly back on my pillows and tucked Wolf and Tiger under my arms. Five minutes later he staggered back, carrying an old wooden tray with a mug of hot chocolate and some toast and Vegemite. "We don't have much in the cupboards. Dad's shopping today, he said."

"That's great, Nicky. Thanks." The first mouthful nearly stuck going down, but after that I ate the toast in huge bites, barely taking the time to chew.

He sat on the end of the bed and swung his feet, a frown on his face. "Sasha, did you see anyone by the falls?"

"How come everyone is asking me that?" I said, too sharply.

"It's not me, it's Dad. He asked me, and I said no, but I heard him talking to another man on the phone."

"And?"

He shrugged. "There's some guy around here who causes trouble. Stealing and getting drunk and –" he lowered his voice to a loud whisper "– smoking marijuana."

I hid my face behind the mug of chocolate, sipping slowly. "Did Dad say who it was? What he looked like?"

"Nah. Dad saw me listening and hung up," Nicky said. "Wanna watch TV?"

"Yeah, why not?" I took my quilt into the family room and settled on the couch. It was almost like being in bed. I was still resting. We watched the news and a lame talk show, and then I let Nicky turn on his Xbox. He played and I drifted off to sleep, waking near dusk. Dad came home and cooked sausages for dinner, and we watched more TV.

Was this going to be life in Manna Creek? Xbox and bad TV every day, every week, every year? Even when one of my favorite shows came on, I couldn't concentrate. It seemed pathetic and over-acted, and irritation grew in me like an itch I wanted to scrape raw with my fingernails.

After sleeping half the day, I wasn't tired, but Dad insisted on lights out by 11 p.m. I lay in bed, blinking up at the stained ceiling. When I turned off my lamp, my room was so dark that the numbers on my little digital clock looked like they were red neon. There were no streetlights here; the one on our old street had shone through my window.

It was like being trapped in an underground cave, and my scalp prickled. Maybe I should leave the light on all night. No, that was being a baby! But the blackness felt thick and suffocating, and my breath started coming in little pants again, and I turned the lamp back on with trembling fingers.

Then I didn't want to close my eyes. *This is ridiculous. I can't lie here all night with my eyes wide open.* But it was a long time before I could force them closed, and even then I lay rigid for ages before I finally drifted off to sleep.

I woke with a jolt and struggled to sit up. My pajama top was soaked with sweat, and I was shivering. Something clung to me like a sticky thread … it was a dream, I knew, but I couldn't remember a single thing in it. Except burning heat against my back. And snow freezing my feet.

It didn't make sense, and I didn't want it to. I swung my legs out of the bed and stood – I had to grab the edge of the windowsill, dizziness swarming around my head. I had to get out of this house, out of this musty stink, out where I could breathe fresh air. But not the back door, no. I headed for the front door, pulling on my jacket, and slipped my feet into my tennis shoes. Weak morning sunlight trickled in, pink and green diamonds, through the stained glass panels. I pushed back the bolt, pulled the door open and stepped onto the porch.

My foot kicked something, and I looked down. "Aarrggh!"

I couldn't move. My scream echoed up and down the street, and behind me, bedsprings creaked and footsteps thumped towards me.

"Sasha? What's the matter? What's wrong? Are you sick?"

At last I could step back, clutching at the door frame. Dad's hair stuck up on end, and his pajamas were buttoned wrongly. I stared at him, but I couldn't unglue my mouth to answer him. All I could do was point down.

Chapter Three

The sheep's head was matted and bloody, its ears half-torn off, its tongue dangling out of its mouth. Its milky eye stared up at me, as if blaming me for what had happened to it.

"Oh, for the love of Pete!" Dad growled. "Where did that come from?"

"From a sheep," Nicky said behind us, making me jump.

"Very funny, Nicholas," Dad said.

In my head, an axe swung in the air. Landed with a grinding thump.

I staggered backwards, tripping over the threshold.

"Come inside," Dad said, catching me and pulling me next to him. He slammed the door and led me into the kitchen, one arm around my shoulders. "I'll make us a strong cup of tea." He kept shaking his head, as if he couldn't quite believe it.

"Who would do that, Dad?" Nicky asked. "Is it a revenge killing?"

I nearly choked, and then a hysterical laugh burst out of me. "For what? Teasing a sheep dog?"

"Now, Sasha, no need for that," Dad said. He turned the faucet on too hard, and water splashed onto his pajama top. "There's no abattoir near here. Maybe …"

"They did it with an axe," I said dully.

"Yes, probably. It was a pretty rough job," Dad said. "But how did you know?"

I ducked my head. How could I explain? "Someone doesn't like us."

"You said only nice people lived here," Nicky piped up.

"I didn't exactly say that," Dad said. "I meant that it was a quiet little town where we're not going to get any big crooks. There's sure to be little ones. Like kids who don't wear their bike helmets, or the odd shoplifter."

"Is that all?" Nicky said.

"Yeah, if I'm lucky," Dad said.

The sheep's head rose up in front of my eyes again, and I swallowed hard, hugging my jacket around me. There was nothing lucky about this town, or the people in it. Dad was hoping for lazy and laid-back; I sensed something that made me want to run. But I had to make the best of it, or I had to

27

at least try. For Dad's sake. I'd promised, and I couldn't let him down.

By mid-afternoon, I was going stir crazy, stuck in the house, pacing, unable to settle with a book or the TV. I felt like a caged wild cat, ready to snarl. Dad was at work, and every time I checked, he was talking to someone new in an endless stream of people going into the police station. It was like everyone from a hundred miles around had come to complain about something, or to meet the new cop.

Nicky had finished his allowed two hours on his Xbox and insisted on practicing his magic tricks on me, even though I'd seen them all a million times. If I had to watch one more piece of rope fail to tie a magic knot, I'd cut it up with a pair of scissors. When I said no for the tenth time, he lost it. "I hate you!"

"Yeah, yeah, whatever," I said. "Let's go for a walk."

"Dad said you've got to stay inside," he said. "You're supposed to be in bed."

"No, he said don't sleep too much. And I rested all day yesterday." My head still ached though, a low-level incessant throb, and sometimes my vision went blurry. "The sun is finally out, and if I have to stay here with you a minute longer, I might do you some damage."

"Stop picking on me."

"Don't hassle me then." The last thing I wanted was a fight with him – he'd run to Dad like he always did, and I'd get the big sister lecture. I needed some space. In Melbourne, I would've caught the bus to the big shopping center and wandered mindlessly for hours, enjoying being nobody. Hopefully, being outside would help get rid of my caged-in feeling.

I put on my boots and my leather jacket and said, "Are you coming or not?"

"Suppose." He followed me out of the house and up the street. "Wonder where Dad put the sheep's head?"

"I don't care, as long as it's nowhere near me." I hadn't looked down as we'd left – even a tiny bit of sheep wool on the porch would've made me sick.

"Where are we going?"

"Dunno. The main street, I guess. Where else is there to go?"

The public bathrooms on the corner were concrete, painted yellow. Not an inspired choice. I imagined myself painting murals along the walls, swirls of color; then I shook my head – I didn't paint anymore. We walked in silence up one side of the main street, stopping at each shop to inspect the windows as if they were the most fascinating sights in the world. The hardware and farm shop had a display of a wood stove and some blocks of firewood. So lifeless. I rubbed the end of my nose and found the cold was making it drip.

"This is boring," Nicky whined.

"Here's a dollar. Go and visit your favorite candy lady."

"Thanks!" He headed to the deli and stopped at the door.

"You want anything?"

I shook my head. I'd planned to stay outside, but a group of kids were in there, and I could imagine what would happen next. They'd know who Nicky was, and they'd hassle him about Dad. Same old, same old. I should watch his back. I pushed open the door, and the bell pinged. Nicky didn't look around, his face pressed to the glass window of the candy counter, but the kids slouching by the magazine racks did. They nudged each other and whispered. Four pairs of eyes zeroed in on me, four faces with sullen expressions. Nobody said hello.

I joined Nicky and pretended to be helping him choose, but I felt their eyes on me, hot and hostile. In my quick check, I'd seen three boys and one girl, about my age, all dressed in jeans and heavy boots. The tallest boy wore a dirty denim jacket. Two had on those flannel shirts that screamed *country*.

"Maybe I'll get raspberries today," Nicky said.

"Hurry up and choose," I whispered.

"Oy, you lot," the woman barked across the shop. "Clear out. And Mark Wallace, if you're not paying for that magazine, put it back before I thump ya."

Out of the corner of my eye, I watched the big, dark-haired boy scowl and pull a magazine out from inside his jacket and put it back on the rack. "Not worth the money," he sneered.

"Good, you won't wanta be coming in here and reading it for free then either," the woman said.

They pushed past Nicky and me, knocking us against each other, on purpose I was sure. I toppled over on the floor, and they laughed; my face flamed. How typical. Why did I ever think a small town would be any different? Cop's kids were fair game.

"You all right, love?" the woman asked.

"Yeah." I brushed down the back of my jeans with angry hands. "You ready, Nicky?"

He paid for his candy, and I checked that the kids weren't waiting outside for us before stepping out onto the sidewalk. The street was empty again, except for two cars up near the art gallery, and I flexed my fingers and tucked them into my pockets. We wandered along, Nicky eating, me trying hard to find something positive about Manna Creek. The next shop was the one called *Magical Moments,* and its window was full of stuff like wishing stones, fairies, dragons and witch's hats. A rack outside the door held some clothes that I flicked through without much interest. It was all tie-dyed cheesecloth and wispy shirts and skirts – hippy stuff might be trendy again, but I hated it. I liked my jeans and leather jacket and my black T-shirts.

"Look at that," Nicky said, pointing to the back of the window display. "They've got magic tricks."

I groaned. "No more, please. Besides, they probably won't have any new ones. You own just about every trick ever made."

"I'm going in to look. Come on." He took my hand and pulled me after him.

The inside of the shop was even more crammed than the window. Every shelf was filled with animal figures and piles of folded clothing and pots and mugs and glasses. Stacks of colored cushions covered the floor space, and silk and velvet curtains hung everywhere. I wandered around, stepping over ceramic elephants and dodging tinkling chimes, and found two purple gauze curtains that would be perfect in my bedroom.

No money. And none until the weekend. Oh, well, maybe they'd still be here then. Manna Creek didn't seem like it was about to have a rush on gauze curtains. The racks of jewelry were tempting, too, and as I fingered the silver Celtic earrings, my eyes kept sliding over to a display of pendants on pink velvet. I moved towards it and glanced over the colored crystals. At the back, a silver pendant set with a polished black stone gleamed like an eye. It drew me and repelled me at the same time, and my hand reached out toward it before I knew what I was doing.

"It's lovely, isn't it?"

I jerked back. A young woman with long dark hair held back by a green sparkly scarf stood right next to me. I hadn't noticed her until that moment. I nodded. "What's the stone?"

"Onyx. You want to try it on?" She smiled at me.

"No, it's OK. I couldn't afford it, so there's no point."

She unpinned the pendant off the velvet and handed it to me. In my palm, it felt incredibly cold, then suddenly it grew warm against my skin. My hand closed around it.

"Ah, you like it," she said. "Here, put it on." She took it out of my hand, ignoring my protests, and fastened it at the back of my neck. The pendant sat against my upper chest, and even through my sweater I could feel it growing warmer.

"There," she said. "Perfect. It must be yours."

"No, I can't," I said. "I have no money."

She smiled, showing small white teeth. "If your parents are close by, they could buy it. A nice souvenir of Manna Creek."

"No, truly, I can't." I fumbled at the catch, suddenly desperate to get the pendant off me. At last it opened, and I handed the onyx back to the woman. "Sorry. We're not tourists. We live here now." I thought she might be offended, but the flash in her eyes was of instant curiosity.

"You must be the new policeman's family," she said. "I'm Tangine. How nice for us to have law and order in town again." She flicked her fingers in the air and smiled gaily, but her tone had an edge of sarcasm. "What else would you like to look at?"

Nicky tugged at my sleeve. "Look, she's got two tricks I don't have yet. Can I buy them? Please?"

"You'll have to ask Dad. He might give you your allowance early." In the corner, the woman lit several incense sticks, and the sweet stink drifted through the air. My vision blurred, and nausea overcame me. I knew I had to get out of there. My stomach lurched and tightened. I raced to the door, nearly tripping over an Indian mat, and made it to the gutter in time to throw up. The tomato soup we had for lunch was utterly gross coming out again and splattered my boots. Funnily

33

enough, as soon as I finished, I felt a hundred times better. Even the ache in my head subsided.

I turned to find Tangine and Nicky staring at me anxiously. She came over and rubbed my shoulder, then put her cool hand on my forehead. "Are you all right?"

"Yeah, I'm good now," I said. "Heaps better. Come on, Nicky, we'll keep walking."

"But –" He shrugged and followed me. "Didn't you like that shop either?"

"It was OK." As we moved away from it, I felt a strange mix of relief and craving to go back. I could still feel the pendant warm against my skin.

"She said she'd keep those tricks for me. Do you think Dad'll say yes?"

"Of course." Dad would say yes to anything that kept us happy here. I quickened my pace and breathed in the crisp air. My head felt clear for the first time in days.

We reached the end of the main street, where the concrete stopped and the gravel started. Across the intersection was the old pub that'd been turned into an art gallery and antique shop. It had been painted a dull apricot color that looked like clay in the winter light. Nicky screwed up his nose. "You don't want to go in there, do you?"

"Why not? I like art and old things." We crossed the street and pushed open the glass-paned door.

Nicky ran his fingers over the doorknob that was in the shape of a lion's head. "Cool."

Inside, a passageway opened out into a large gallery with white walls. The carpet was old and tattered, with a pattern that reminded me of what I'd just thrown up. In one corner, a gray cat with long fur and a twitching tail lay curled up on a cushion. Paintings of all shapes and sizes hung along the walls, and there were several free-standing sculptures.

We circled slowly, and I wondered how many of the paintings were done by local artists. There were lots of pictures of gum trees and rocks and hills, and one that I recognized as Bungaloo Falls, even though the artist had titled it "Blue Days." Along one wall was a series of very weird paintings of jumbled images: a clown on a shelf with rain clouds dribbling on him; a service station with soldiers instead of gas pumps; an old woman with a towel around her surrounded by boxes of cereal. They weren't just weird, they were also artistically terrible. Flat and lifeless.

"I could do better than this," Nicky whispered, a little too loudly.

"Could you now?" said a harsh voice behind us.

We both jumped, and turned. "I meant … I thought …" Nicky flushed and stammered.

"I doubt you thought at all, boy," said the man. "And you're hardly an art critic now, are you?"

"No," Nicky said, in a small voice.

I put my hand on his shoulder and straightened my spine; we were allowed an opinion, and besides, the paintings really were awful.

The man's thick red moustache bristled. "And of course you're here to buy something?" he said sarcastically.

"We're looking around," I said, as snootily as I could. "Dad might like something for our new house, if we find something suitable."

"I doubt it," he muttered. "Fine, look around then. Don't touch anything."

He sat down behind an antique-looking desk and began flipping the pages of a glossy magazine, glaring at us every now and then.

"Let's go," Nicky whispered.

"I haven't seen everything yet." I wasn't going to let him chase us out. I kept walking along the walls, and near his desk, there was a row of four paintings that were a million times better than anything else. As I checked the signatures, I felt his eyes spearing my back. Two paintings were by Arthur Boyd, and the other two were by people who sounded familiar. We'd just done Australian art at my old school and spent a day at the National Gallery.

Were these genuine? They sure had big price tags. The two Boyds were $40,000 each, and the others were $29,000 and $14,000. No wonder the place had bars on all the windows. I glanced up and spotted security cameras in two corners. An art magazine was displayed on the corner table, open to a double-page ad for this gallery. Maybe this town attracted more tourists than I thought. I sneaked a look at the man – he was watching me intently, and my skin crawled. Time to leave.

Nicky was inspecting a sculpture made out of cutlery welded together and sprayed fluorescent green. I whispered, "Seen enough?" He nodded, and we escaped into the cold street.

"Some of that stuff was really bad," Nicky said. "That knife and fork thing was eight hundred dollars! Who would pay that?"

"Don't know. Those paintings near his desk were the real thing, though."

"Really?"

"They had huge price tags. You wouldn't pay that for a copy."

"Guess what?" Nicky leaned in close. "You know the worst paintings? The ones we were looking at when he yelled at me?"

"Yeah."

"He painted them."

"How do you know that?"

"Because his name was on them, and his name was on the brochures as the gallery owner." Nicky put on a fake snooty voice. "Arthur Jones-Sutton, at your service. *Not.*" We both burst into laughter and giggled all the way home.

Chapter Four

Two police vehicles were parked outside our house – a four-wheel drive and a sedan, both in glaring blue and white. Dad had said he was getting a 4 x 4, but this was huge, with a menacing bull bar on the front.

Inside, we found Dad drinking coffee and talking to two men in police uniform. Neither of them looked familiar, but their faces were friendly. Not here about a crime, then.

"Sash, where have you been?" Dad said sternly. "I thought you promised to stay inside."

"I needed some fresh air," I said. "I'm feeling better, truly."

"Make sure you don't overdo it." He gestured to the other men. "This is Mario Costa, and that's my old mate, Paul

Kane. They brought up my new vehicle. Did you see it?"

"Couldn't really miss it," I said. "Do you need a truck license to drive it?"

"Ha-ha," Dad said. "Paul's brought you both something, too."

I looked around. "Brought us what?" What could two policemen possibly give me? Apart from another warning?

Paul smiled. "He's in the family room. Go and say hello."

Nicky raced ahead of me; I was trying to be cool, but my feet sped up of their own accord. I was only two seconds behind him, but already Nicky had his arms wrapped around a large German shepherd with thick toffee-brown and black fur. It sat on its haunches, alert, but tolerating Nicky's hug. Two soft brown eyes regarded me, two furry ears twitched slightly. I knew a silly grin was spreading across my face, but I couldn't stop it. I didn't want to. "Don't strangle him," I told Nicky.

"He's too tough for that," Nicky said. "He's fantastic, isn't he? I can't believe it."

Nice kid. House is cold.

Dad, Paul and Mario crowded in behind me. "I've had him for a year," Paul said, "but we're moving to an apartment with no yard, and I can't keep him. You can see he's good with kids."

"What's his name?" Nicky asked.

"King. But that was his working name. You can call him something different, if you want."

"I like King," Nicky said.

"He's Sasha's dog, too," Dad said. "Don't you think you'd better check with her first?"

I said *King* inside my head a couple of times and nodded. "That's an OK name." The dog's nose bobbed up.

Glad you like it. Turn the heater on.

"Is someone cold?" I asked. I bent and patted the dog's head, loving the feel of his soft fur.

"Not me," Paul said. "You'll need to make sure he gets plenty of exercise. He's used to training every day. I'll give you his toys before I go."

"He was a police dog?" I asked.

"Yes. He did well until his final tests, then he spooked and hid behind his trainer. He can't stand the sound of a gun firing."

Nicky said, "Sit," and King sat on his foot. I could've sworn the dog smiled.

I asked Dad, "How come we're getting a dog?"

He rubbed his nose. "Well, the main reason we've never had pets before is because of your mother. She was allergic. So now …"

Now that she'd gone forever, we could do what we liked. "Good," I said. "I'd rather have a dog anyway."

"Sasha!" Dad said.

"What else do we need to know?" I asked Paul.

"He's never had canned food, so no need to start now," he said. "Otherwise you'll have smelly dog poop everywhere.

A good dry food and your leftovers as a treat will be plenty, along with lots of fresh water. He doesn't like the cold much, so he'll hog the heater if you have it on. Don't let him get too close to it. And don't let him sleep on your bed. He weighs a ton."

Dad grinned. "That'll be the hardest rule to abide by, knowing these two."

Nicky was testing out more of King's training, telling him to lie down and roll over. When King followed all his commands, Nicky's face glowed. "This dog is so cool!"

Cool. Interesting.

Right then, I realized that the deep, quiet voice I kept hearing wasn't one of the policemen – it was in my head. A hundred tiny hooks dug into my scalp and pulled tight. Where was the voice coming from? Was it me? Was I going crazy?

No, it's me.

I glanced wildly around, but the only eyes looking back at me were King's. That wasn't possible. It couldn't be possible! Dizziness swept over me in a wave, and I put out my hand. Dad grabbed at it, helping me to sit. "Sasha, time for you to rest again. You've been doing too much."

I didn't argue. I curled up on my bed under my quilt, like a snail retreating to safety, scrunching my eyes shut, trying to blank my mind. But the voice had gone, and I slowly calmed. I must have imagined it. I *did* imagine it.

I could hear the men talking in the kitchen, about police

work and families and football. Dad sounded so nostalgic that tears filled my eyes. Had he really wanted to come here? Or had he done it for our sakes? Maybe we all thought we were here for each other, when in fact no one wanted to leave Melbourne.

No, Dad had been really keen right from the start, when the possibility of a posting here had come up. He'd been brought up in the country, on a dairy farm, and he'd told us he would love the chance to go back.

For a few seconds, I allowed myself to wonder if Mum would've changed her mind and stayed with us if she'd known about Manna Creek. About all the changes Dad was prepared to make for us. But that was pathetic, thinking like that. Mum didn't care about anyone but herself, and a move to the country wouldn't have changed that. I pushed her out of my head.

I dozed for a while, soothed by the rhythm of their voices, and when I woke up, King was sitting next to my bed, his muzzle resting on the quilt. "Hello," I said.

Hello. Are you feeling better?

A tiny jolt of fear zapped through me, and I stared at him. He didn't talk. Dogs don't talk. Maybe my brain had been injured more than they'd thought, and I was hallucinating. That had to be it. I was imagining things. Like the greasy-haired man.

No, you saw him.

"What? How do you know?" Now *I* was talking to this

dog? This was getting worse. I rubbed my temple with two fingers, digging into the hollow. I hated how my hands trembled, but I couldn't stop them.

You'll get used to me. The boss said someone saw that man walking away from the falls.

This was hopeless. This was out of my control. I didn't want to hear this voice. I could hardly breathe. I needed someone sane in the room. "Dad!" I yelled.

"What's the matter?" Dad rushed into my room, his face flushed. "You feel sick? You want me to take the dog out?"

"No, I'm OK." I struggled upright, keeping an eye on King. He watched me attentively. It was like a standoff. "Do you think ..."

"What?" His forehead creased. "Tell me what the problem is."

I couldn't. There was no way to explain it. My mouth opened and shut again, the words glued to the back of my brain. If this was like before ...

"There's something special you want for dinner?" Dad believed nutritious food fixed nearly everything. I leaped on the diversion.

"Yeah, some of your chili would be good."

Don't offer me any leftovers.

I glanced at King. His tongue was poking out in a doggy grin. "You're kidding."

"Pardon?" Dad said, confused.

Oh, no. "No, that wasn't what I meant," I said. "Look, I'm

sorry for being a pain and getting hurt on my first day here. I know it was the last thing you needed."

If I refused to look at the dog again, this voice thing might stop.

"It's not like you did it on purpose," Dad said. "It was an accident. I'll start the chili right now. You want to get up and watch the news?"

"In a minute." I perched on the side of my bed and slowly reached out my hand, like I was about to touch an electric wire. I rested my palm on King's head. He felt like a normal dog – rough, warm, smelly. I could hear him breathing as he sat perfectly still beside me. A sense of calm stole over me. I was tempted to say something to him in my head, but it felt dangerous, like teetering on the edge of a cliff. I stood up, letting my hand drop, and King lay down, his nose on his paws. Had I offended him? No, I wasn't going to let myself think like that!

I put my bathrobe on over my clothes and found my fluffy chicken slippers. For once, they failed to cheer me up. In the family room, the gas heater was on, and the room felt cozy. Nicky sat on the floor, his magic tricks spread out around him.

"Hey, about time," he said. "I've been practicing my coin tricks. I think I've finally got this one right."

King padded in behind me. I ignored him, giving Nicky my full attention, even though I'd seen this trick fail at least twenty times.

Nicky put the dollar coin on the coffee table and went through his routine. "And now, the coin has disappeared!" And it kind of had.

"Wow, that's great, Nick," I said, pretending I couldn't see it in his lap.

"Yeah, I just have to work out how to get it back now."

I sat on the couch and watched the news, while Dad hovered near the doorway, one eye on the dinner he was cooking. King lay near the heater, his nose on his paws again, like he was waiting. Or sulking. His eyes were closed, so I spent a few moments inspecting him. Tail, ears, four legs, teeth. See, he was just an ordinary dog.

I am ordinary. It's just that you listen properly.

"What do you mean?" I asked, startled.

"I didn't say anything," Nicky said.

Dad sat next to me, gently smoothing my hair off my face. "Are you sure you're feeling OK? Is your head still hurting?"

"My head's fine," I said. "I was daydreaming, that's all." It was time to change the subject. The laptop sat on the coffee table, unopened. "When are you going to connect our computer to the Internet, Dad?"

"They're coming tomorrow," Dad said. "We've had to change providers, so you'll both get new email addresses, I'm afraid. You'll have to let all your friends know."

Yeah, right. All one of them. The only person who was still speaking to me before we'd left the city was my cousin, Skye. All my other so-called friends had dumped me, either because

45

I'd gotten them into trouble, or their parents had decided I was a bad influence. I hadn't even been driving the stolen car. It wasn't like I'd robbed a bank!

Humph. You're a policeman's daughter. You should know better. King's ears twitched, and I glared at him.

Shut up. You know nothing about it!

King let out a big sigh and rolled over. *So, have you decided you're not going crazy yet?*

"Listen, don't you …" I trailed off when Nicky and Dad both stared at me. "Don't you think the chili will be done by now? I'm starving." I smiled brightly at them and ignored King's little rowf. *Leave me alone, dog.*

"Yep, nearly ready," Dad said. "I want to watch the weather first."

We ate in front of the TV, a habit that we'd never had when Mum was around. Now, the plate of buttered bread on the coffee table annoyed me. It was like Mum-not-there was affecting how we lived as much as Mum-there. Tomorrow, I'd suggest we eat at the table again.

"I'll have some time off in the morning," Dad said. "Do you want to go for a drive? Have a look around?"

"Can we take King?" Nicky asked.

Good idea. Get the lay of the land.

I ignored him. Did I want to see more of this place? Did I want to give it a chance? "Where will we go? Into Marberry?" It was the nearest big town, about twenty miles away.

"No, around here," Dad said. "Up in the hills. There are

46

lots of large houses with amazing gardens, and a winery where we can have lunch. I might buy myself a couple of bottles of nice red."

"Houses?" Nicky said. "Why would we want to look at houses?"

Dad looked down at his plate, poking at a kidney bean. "Actually, I want to go and look around. There are a lot of weekend places up there, expensive ones, and apparently there've been a few break-ins and burglaries lately."

"Da-a-ad," we chorused. That was typical of him – combining work with an outing. But I didn't mind. I liked the sound of hills and gardens, and it'd be good to get out of Manna Creek.

I read for ages after I went to bed – one of my books I'd brought with me, a fantasy novel. I'd read it before, but it didn't matter. The story took me away to another world, one where characters worked out their problems and helped each other and became better people along the way. That would never happen to me. The trouble label was stuck to me so well that I didn't know how to peel it off. In the city, no one would give me a chance to change, or even prove I was trying to be good. Except Dad. Good old Dad. A hug from him on a bad day kept me from crumbling under the weight of everyone's contempt.

Maybe moving here would prove Dad was a secret genius.

King had gone to bed with Nicky, lying on the floor, but now he pushed open my door and came in, sitting next to my bed.

"Hey," I said. "You won't fit on here with me."

I don't sleep on beds!

Oh, right, you're tough.

He didn't reply, just lay down and closed his eyes. I stepped over him and went to the bathroom, then decided I should try to sleep. I didn't want to admit it, but with him in my room, I felt better about closing my eyes.

Something jolted me awake, and it took a few seconds to realize I'd heard breaking glass. Had something fallen in the kitchen? Or … was the sheep's head back? King was by my door, whining to be let out. I jumped out of bed and opened the door – he trotted to the front door and barked once. I hesitated, biting my lip, and he scratched at the door and whined again. *Hurry, let me out.* I opened it for him, and he raced outside, disappearing down the dark street.

"King!" I shouted. "Come back."

Can't. I'm chasing him.

"What's going on?" Dad said. He switched on the hallway light.

"King's chasing someone."

"Shoot," Dad said. "I'd better go after him. Who's he chasing? Why?"

I turned on the light in the family room. The front window was broken, and a rock sat in the middle of the floor. As I gaped at it, chilled air wrapped freezing fingers around me. "Someone chucked a rock through our window."

"Did they now?" Dad quickly went and pulled on his

police sweater and trousers and grabbed his keys off the hook by the door. "Lock the door after me. Keep Nicky inside." He pulled the door shut after him, and the police 4 x 4 roared into life, leaving me standing there, shivering, arms tightly crossed against my chest. Where on earth had King gone? Was he OK? I secured the double locks on both doors, put on my bathrobe and slippers and checked on Nicky. He was still fast asleep, his arms flung over his head. I tucked them under his quilt and then tested the front and back door locks again. When I thought I heard rustling outside, my heartbeat thundered in my ears. I froze, holding my breath, praying I'd imagined it, and the silence grew back thickly around me. I shook my head. Time to put the kettle on.

While I waited for it to boil, I found one of our packing boxes and cut a square of cardboard for the broken window pane, taping it across the hole. Busy work. I left the rock where it was – Dad would want to check it out as evidence. But it had been more than twenty minutes, and neither Dad nor King had returned. Where were they?

I sat hunched over my hot chocolate at the kitchen table, trying not to think the worst, but black thoughts snaked through my mind. Maybe the rock thrower was sneaking back to our house again, while Dad was driving away. Maybe they had a gun, or a knife. Maybe there'd been a confrontation, and someone had been shot. I sipped some hot chocolate, trying to soothe my dread.

For the first time, I had a glimmer of understanding of

what Mum had meant when she said the waiting and the not-knowing was the worst. It ate away at you until you couldn't stand it anymore. I checked to make sure Dad's mobile number was still on the fridge. Should I call him? How long should I wait? What would I do if he didn't come back? I kept sitting, frozen in my seat, until my chocolate was cold, listening to the clock on the wall ticking.

Chapter Five

I could hardly believe it when I heard the rumble of Dad's 4 x 4 outside at last, his headlights flashing past the front window. My limbs felt like they'd seized up, and it was an effort to stand. A jabbing pain in my back reminded me sharply that I had bruises there, too, even if I couldn't see them. I unlocked the door and let Dad in, and King followed, panting, his tongue hanging out. Dad filled his water bowl and gave him a big pat. "Good boy, King. Good boy."

I didn't catch him. Not good.

"What happened?" I snapped. Now that they were home safe, I was mad at them for being away so long and frightening me. "You were gone for ages."

"Whoever it was had a car waiting in the next street. King was chasing it, I think. I saw the tire marks where it took off in a hurry. I caught up with him about four miles out of town."

Good thing, too. I didn't feel like walking all the way back.

I hid a smile. "Do you know who it was?"

"No," Dad said. "You didn't touch that rock, did you?"

"Would I do something like that?" I said.

He squeezed my arm. "Guess some of that procedural stuff has rubbed off on you, eh?"

"I fixed the window with some cardboard."

"Good girl. Thanks."

Dad's praise warmed me. "Why would someone do that? And the sheep's head, too?" I shuddered. "They must really hate us."

"There's been no policeman here for six months or more, so the local crooks have pretty much done what they like. It's someone trying to scare us off."

"They're hardly likely to scare *you* off!"

Or me.

He frowned. "I'm more worried about you and Nicky. You'd better stick together from now on, until I catch this person. Make sure you take King with you everywhere."

As I realized what he meant, the skin tightened across my shoulders. "Is that why you got King? Did you know someone would threaten us?"

"No, of course not." He sounded astonished, and I wanted to believe him. "Paul needed a good home for him, so it seemed like the perfect solution."

"It is, Dad. Honestly." Even if I *was* going crazy, thinking the dog was talking to me.

You'll get over it.

We all went back to bed, and King lay beside my bed again, but this time he stayed alert, ears up, nose pointing to the door. In the morning, Dad played down the broken window to Nicky so he wouldn't be scared, and he'd already removed the rock to send for fingerprinting, on the off-chance they'd find something on its smoother edges. We were ready to leave for our outing when Dad's mobile rang, and his face creased into its serious police business frown.

"I'll be there shortly," he said, pressing the disconnect button.

"Guess we're staying home," I said.

"No, you two can come," Dad said. "As long as you stay in the car it'll be OK. There's been a break-in, but the caretaker doesn't know if they stole anything. I need to check it out before I call the detectives in from Marberry."

Maybe Dad didn't want to leave us home on our own, but I didn't want that either. The cardboard I'd taped over the window was way too flimsy. Dad opened the back of the 4 x 4, and King jumped in.

"Why can't he ride on the back seat with me?" Nicky said.

"Police dogs like being in the back," Dad told him. "Part of their training."

The main road wound up into the hills, with lots of smaller

side roads and long driveways. Dad was right about some of
the houses being huge, but not like the ugly McMansions
in Melbourne's new housing areas. Here, they were historic,
two-story places, with lots of windows and long wraparound
porches, the kind of second home Dad said belonged to the
very rich. The gardens were full of huge leafy trees, bushes and
orderly flowers, and I glimpsed the occasional pond or dam.
Behind their big iron gates, most of the houses looked deserted.

We turned in at a driveway where the double gates were
open, drove along a narrow road and parked near a high
dark-green hedge that screened the house from the road.

"Whose house is this?" I asked.

"A man called Connor Jacobson. He's not here often, from
what I know. And it's way too secluded," Dad said. "No one
can see what's going on. You kids stay in the car. I don't want
you wandering around while I'm here on a call."

He headed to the large double front doors and pressed
the doorbell with a long jab. One door opened, and he
disappeared inside.

"This guy must be rich," Nicky said. "I can see a tennis
court over there, past the trees."

"Imagine having this place as a weekend home," I said,
counting windows. "I'll bet that house has at least six bedrooms."

"Maybe they have a heated pool. Maybe we can come up
and swim in it."

"As if! They wouldn't let us within a million miles of their
pool if they had one." I craned my neck. "Look – over there,

by the pond. It's a little kangaroo."

"Cool," Nicky said. "No, that's a wallaby. It's darker, see? And smaller. I'm going to see if I can get close to it." He opened his door.

Tell him to stay in the car.

"Nicky! Dad'll be really mad if you go running around." I leaned over and pulled on his jacket. "He'll take us straight home again."

"Oh, all right." He slammed the door and sulked.

Dad was inside the house for a long, boring twenty minutes. Nicky stopped sulking and patted King for a while, then bounced around on the back seat, watching for wallabies. I didn't talk to King, and he stayed out of my head. Maybe he was giving me time to think. Finally, Dad emerged from the house, looking thoughtful, and got into the 4 x 4. "I need to make a call and then check in on a couple of people."

Nicky and I made faces at each other as Dad punched numbers into his phone. "Won't be long."

"Yeah, right." As I focused on the house again, the curtains in the window next to the front door twitched. We were being watched. Why?

Nobody likes the police hanging around.

I jumped and looked over my shoulder. King sat in the back, and his eyes met mine. *At least you're paying attention.*

I stuck my tongue out at him, glad Nicky was scanning the garden for the wallaby.

Dad finished his call to the detective sergeant in Marberry

and snapped his phone shut. "It'll take them a couple of hours to get here. They have to wait for a tech. I hope Colin Parker doesn't start calling me to complain."

"Who's he?" Nicky asked.

"The caretaker. He does the gardens, too. Jacobson is in Bali on vacation." He started the engine. "The nearest neighbors might've noticed something."

"Too many trees," I said. "Plus that hedge."

"Yes, but a strange car on the road or someone walking would stand out around here." He drove further up the winding road and turned into another entrance. This time the gates were closed. "Nicky, open these for us, please?"

"Why can't Sasha do it?"

"Sasha has to take it easy today, remember? Come on."

It was fun being waited on for a change, but I knew it wouldn't last. I sat quietly while Nicky unhooked the latch, pushed the gates wide and climbed back in. "It's freezing out there," he grumbled.

"The forecast is for snow in the mountains," Dad said.

"We could go skiing," Nicky said.

We drove down a narrow track between the thick hedges that seemed to be everywhere and came out into a graveled circle that was dotted with weeds. The house was amazing, like a fairytale cottage, two stories high, with little balconies and mullioned windows. "Is this another weekend place?" I asked.

"No, Mrs. Alsopp lives here. She's a local legend, has been

here since she was born." Dad pulled up next to a statue of an angel with outstretched wings.

"Yuck," I said. "That looks like it belongs in a cemetery."

The front door opened, and a tiny old woman with a pink shawl around her shoulders came out and stood at the top of the steps. "Good morning, officer," she called.

"At least she's friendly," Dad murmured. He got out and galloped up the steps to shake her hand. "Hello. I'm Senior Constable Miller."

"Come in and have a cup of tea," she said, beaming. "And bring your children. They are yours, aren't they?"

Nicky was out of the car before she finished speaking. "I'm Nicky. And that's Sasha."

I went to join them on the porch, but King seemed happy to stay in the car, snoozing. At the top of the steps, I pulled my jacket tightly around me as the cold air bit, then turned to gaze across the garden. Statues of animals and people were dotted everywhere, and there were two enormous ponds full of waterlilies. A large, circular garden of pruned rose bushes promised a colorful display in the spring. I wasn't really into gardens, but this was the kind of place that would have secret trails and great places to hide away from everyone. "Wow, it's amazing," I said.

"Thank you, dear," Mrs. Alsopp said. "It's a bit much for one person, but I have a very good gardener, who does as he is instructed." She sounded like one of those old ladies who looked sweet and dainty, but had a skeleton made of steel.

"Come in," she said, and we followed her down a long hallway lined with paintings of all shapes and sizes. Most of them were very old, of people with funny hair and long dresses, or dusty landscapes. All the doors were closed except one; I poked my head into the room and saw more paintings and lots of antique furniture and vases and plates. The house was like a museum.

At the end of the hallway was a large, bright kitchen and a wooden table and chairs. Dad and Nicky went in and pulled chairs out from the table, but I hesitated in the doorway and looked back, catching a flicker of something out of the corner of my eye. Was there someone behind me? Had one of those closed doors opened for a moment, or had I imagined it?

I stood there, wanting to go back and look, and an uneasy feeling crawled over me. A faint red haze clouded my vision, and warmth pushed towards me down the hallway, even though it was chilly and damp. Maybe there was a fire burning in one of the rooms, but how could I feel it if the doors were shut? I shivered, unable to go forward or back.

"Come in and sit down, dear," Mrs. Alsopp called, and it was as if she'd snapped the grip of whatever held me. I stepped into the kitchen and sat next to Dad, near the old wood stove. It was burning busily, a pot of soup bubbling on the top, and the tang of wood smoke hovered in the air.

"Would you children like some cookies?"

"Yes, please," Nicky said, before Dad could stop him.

"Er, I'm actually here on a bit of business," Dad said.

"Oh, yes?" She bustled around, filling the kettle and getting plates out of a cupboard. I watched her closely, wondering what the weird sensation in the hallway had been about. Was this old woman ... I shook my head. It couldn't be *that* again. It couldn't.

"Several of your neighbors have had break-ins, and a number of paintings have been stolen." Dad got out his notebook. "Have you seen anyone around, a stranger perhaps, or a local who wouldn't normally be up this way? Or any strange cars on the road?"

She laughed. "Good gracious, no. The wall around the garden is about eight feet high, you know, and I rarely go out these days. Shopping once a week, that's it for me."

"Is there anyone else living here?" Dad asked.

"No, just me. My daughter, Jacqueline, comes to visit every month or two, and stays overnight. That's all."

I wondered if she was lonely. I couldn't imagine never seeing a single person for days on end.

"Who does your garden?" Dad asked, and took down the person's name and number. "You need to make sure you keep your house locked up. Whoever is doing these burglaries knows the area, I think. They're targeting specific houses where there are things of value."

"I do have an alarm system, young man," she said. "I'm not completely ga-ga."

"Oh, no, I didn't mean that," Dad said, his face turning red.

Nicky giggled, and Dad glared at him. I smelled the delicious sweet, chocolaty cookies she'd put on the table and reached for one. Maybe everything was OK here.

"How do you take your tea?" she asked us, and poured cups of a dark brew, offering milk and sugar. The cookies were double chocolate chip, homemade, and Nicky and I ate three each while Mrs. Alsopp told us about the history of her house.

"My father added the extensions," she said. "And the stables at the back were pulled down – I've never liked horses. My husband died ten years ago, and since then it's been quite a battle to keep the house shipshape."

"It's very damp and cold up here," Dad said. "I've been told there's a lot of fog in the winter."

"That's true." She gazed around the brightly furnished kitchen with its red curtains and tablecloth. "I spend most of my time in the kitchen these days. Or the living room. Both have open fires, and a good stack of wood keeps me going for months."

"Why don't you put the heater on?" Nicky asked, pointing at a small fan heater in the corner.

"Jacqueline bought me that," Mrs. Alsopp said. "I hate the thing. It vibrates and makes the room too stuffy. I just leave it there to keep her happy."

She told us more stories about the house and the town and what it was like fifty years ago before all the "rich city folk moved in," her face crinkling as she laughed. Finally Dad said he had to talk to more neighbors, and we escaped. I touched each of the doors in the hallway as we walked out, but they were cold. I'm just being stupid, I thought.

King sat up as we returned to the 4 x 4, but he seemed intent on Mrs. Alsopp, who waved us off from the top of the steps. I waited, but he didn't say anything to me. In the end, I asked, *Is something wrong?*

She's very isolated here. I hope she locks her doors.

She says she does.

I could tell Dad wasn't happy about leaving her there alone either, but short of camping on her lawn, what more could we do? We drove through the entrance, and Nicky got out to close the gates. "I don't think she has many people to talk to," I said to Dad.

"Poor old thing," Dad said. "I bet she's refused to move into a retirement home because of that house. It'll get the better of her, though. Half the guttering is rusted out, and quite a few boards are rotten."

Nicky jumped back into the car. "She makes good cookies. Where are we going now?"

"The neighbor on the other side – James Beer," Dad said. "If he's home, that is."

After winding around a dozen corners, we reached the next house, a large, brick house with white columns. The big iron gates were padlocked, and Dad came back to the 4 x 4. "Thought so. He'll be in Melbourne. I'll need to find his number and call him."

"Why? If he's not here, he won't have seen anyone," I said.

"Yes, but he should be warned – his property could

be next." Dad accelerated down the road to the bridge. "Now, let's check out this lunch place that Mrs. Sullivan recommended."

"Mrs. Who?"

"The lady who organized our house cleaning when we arrived. She works at the post office. Seems to know everything and everyone."

I used my sleeve to wipe the condensation off my window. "Life in the country. Does everyone know about our sheep's head and broken glass, too?"

Dad frowned. "No. And don't you tell anyone. I might catch someone off guard that way, if they know something they shouldn't."

I shivered. A dead sheep and a rock through the window. What was coming next?

Nothing. I'll be watching.

Was it the greasy-haired man?

Don't know. Stop worrying.

I settled back in my seat and focused on the landscape of rolling hills and bush, with distant green fields. Soon, we climbed up another winding road and found the winery Mrs. Sullivan had told Dad about. The restaurant was made of stone and wooden beams, with wide glass windows looking out over the rocky valley. Behind the buildings were vast acres of grape vines, all bare sticks at this time of the year.

Dad rubbed his hands. "They make a good shiraz here, I'm told."

At last, my headache was down to a small twinge, and now I was starving. Dad and Nicky both had lamb chops and I ate my way through a huge steak and a pile of crisp chips. Yum.

"Can I give my bones to King?" Nicky asked.

"No, cooked bones like that aren't good for dogs," Dad said. "I brought dog food and water – do you want to go and give him some?"

"Sure." Nicky raced outside, and Dad raised his eyebrows at me.

"You put away that steak without any trouble. Feeling better?"

I nodded. "How many robberies have there been?"

"Five so far. Four before I arrived, so I have to get up to speed on them as well." He pulled at his tight waistband and sighed, leaning back. "I do love it when someone else cooks for us."

"Don't look at me," I said. "I can make sandwiches, that's all."

"How about some cooking lessons?"

I made a face. Mum used to cook, and offered to show me, but I'd never been interested. Too busy painting and drawing. But I didn't want to go there. "Is it one person doing all the robberies?"

"No evidence either way yet. The caretaker heard a noise early this morning, and when he checked, he found the back door forced open."

"What was stolen? Money?"

Dad waved to a waitress and asked for coffee, then turned back to me. "No, nothing. He thinks he frightened them off. Why are you so curious? You haven't been interested in my police job for quite a while."

Not since I started getting arrested myself. I shrugged. "The robberies are the most exciting thing that's happened around here. Have you been and talked to that guy who owns the gallery at the end of the main street?"

"Not yet. Why?"

"He's weird. Nicky and I went in to have a look around, and he acted like we were going to steal something."

"I believe some of the paintings that've been stolen over the past couple of months were bought from his gallery." Dad sipped his hot coffee. "Mmm, I know where to come when I need a decent dose of caffeine."

"Have you got any suspects?"

"Not a one. The Marberry detectives think it might be a gang from Melbourne, coming up and using someone local for information. Has to be a local involved – how else would they know when people are away?"

"Could be Mrs. Sullivan then," I said. "She knows everything."

Dad laughed out loud, and I realized how long it'd been since I'd heard that sound. Weeks and weeks. Months. Our family had been in a black hole for so long, and now Dad was laughing, and outside Nicky raced King past the big windows

64

and threw a ball for him, his face alight with happiness.

And me? My life still felt like a whirlpool of debris, and I wasn't sure whether I was being sucked into the middle or slowly swimming out to the edge. But I decided one thing as I watched Dad sip his coffee and hum under his breath – I wanted to keep that cheerful look on Dad's face, even if it meant learning to cook.

Chapter Six

"We have to take King for a long walk today," Nicky said over breakfast. "Dad said he needs plenty of exercise, and he's bought us a bag of tennis balls for King to play with."

"King can't play tennis," I said, munching cornflakes. "He couldn't hold the racquet properly."

Very funny. King huffed in the corner of the family room, lying in his usual spot next to the heater.

"No, he chases the tennis balls," Nicky explained patiently.

"Why does he need a whole bag full?"

"He chews them up pretty fast, Dad said."

"Later." I rubbed my face and yawned. "Let me wake up first."

Nicky grinned. "You'd better practice getting up early this week. You have to start catching the school bus next Monday."

"Don't remind me." I ruffled his hair; it was guaranteed to annoy him. "Just because you get to walk around the corner to the local school."

"Yep. Mrs. Sullivan said there's only four kids in Grade Five this year. I'll be Number Five." He tried to do a handstand against the back door and toppled over, crashing into the wall.

"You make a hole, Dad'll put you in jail." I spooned up the last of the cornflakes from my bowl and thought about toast. Maybe later. And I'd think about school on Sunday night, if I really had to. It was a few days away yet. The high school was in Marberry, and the bus left Manna Creek at 8 a.m. I was used to a five-minute walk to school, not a half-hour bus trip, picking up kids along the way. I was dreading it. For all the obvious reasons. New kid, cop's daughter. And if the gossip network had been busy, everyone would know I'd only been here one day and ended up in the hospital. So I'd be the dumb city slicker, too. I sighed.

"Hurry up," said Nicky. "How awake do you have to be?"

"I have to have a shower, at least."

"Dad said take it easy on the water."

"Yeah, yeah." Surely I could finally take the dressing off the back of my head? I eased it away, wincing as it pulled some of my hair out, and jumped in the shower. The hot water was bliss, and I risked washing the front of my hair, but I didn't touch the stitches. After I'd dried myself and dressed, I found a hand mirror so I could check the back of my head.

"Arrrgghhhh!"

"What? What?" Nicky came running, his face white. "Are you sick? Are you gonna faint?"

"My hair!" I screamed. "They shaved the back of my head! I look like a freak!"

"Yeah. So?" Nicky peered at where I was pointing. "How else were they going to put stitches and stuff in?"

"I'll have to wear a hat for weeks. I look like the bride of Frankenstein."

He giggled, and I pulled his ear. "Ow! It's not my fault."

"You laughed." Everyone would laugh. I tried to comb my hair over the bare patch – it was huge, and my hair was too short. Disaster! I'd have to wear a hat to that stupid school.

It's only a bit of fur. It'll grow back.

"How would you like me to shave your tail?" I yelled.

"Huh? I don't have a tail," Nicky said.

"Never mind!" I stormed off to my bedroom and hunted through my clothes, searching for a Bulldogs beanie I knew was there somewhere. Nothing. It must be out in the shed in a box. I pulled on jeans and a warm sweater, found my tennis shoes and headed out to the stack of boxes with my name on them. The back door swung open, I marched down the steps and immediately felt dizzy, but I was too angry to let it get the better of me. How could they *shave* a huge patch off my head?

I found the beanie, but also another hat someone had given me that I'd forgotten about. A blue and white Laplander

68

hat with ear flaps. That'd do, and it'd keep my head and ears warm. Manna Creek was freezing, closer to the mountains than I'd realized; I wouldn't be surprised if it snowed soon.

I pulled the shed door closed, and the nausea rose up again. What was going on? Had someone sprayed the backyard with weed killer, and I was allergic? Back inside the house, the nausea faded slowly, and I stared out of the kitchen window. The shed was made of sheets of iron, a bit rusted here and there, nothing special. But when I looked across at the derelict building in the other corner of the yard, every muscle in my body tensed. Holes in the stone walls, the window frame rotted and broken, half of the old iron roof gone. Ivy had grown up one side, but someone had cleared it away, leaving a cobweb of old roots and dead suckers that was being taken over by blackberry sprouts. There was no door, only a doorway with a frame made out of rough slabs of wood.

For a moment, my vision blurred, and I saw a flash of red. Without realizing, I'd slapped both hands over my mouth to stop a whimper slipping out.

"Watcha looking at?"

I jumped, my heart thumping double-speed, my hands flying down to hold on tight to the edge of the sink before I toppled over. "Don't creep up on me like that!"

"I didn't. Did I, King?" Nicky had his hand on King's collar, but King was staring at me.

What's the matter?

"What is that disgusting wreck in our backyard?" I choked

out. "It looks like something out of a horror movie. Someone should've knocked it down years ago. Before it falls down." I wanted to run outside and attack it with a sledgehammer.

"Can't," Nicky said. "Dad said it was a historical building, the cell attached to the old original police station. The historical society is gonna restore it."

I swallowed hard, but the lump in my throat stayed there. "It's gross."

"It's neat-o. It's probably got ghosts in it."

"What? Who said?"

He shrugged. "Nobody. I just reckon it would, that's all."

King nudged my leg with his nose. *Problem?*

There's something wrong in there. Bad. I shuddered and rubbed roughly at my eyes. "Let's take King out for tennis. I need some fresh air."

We headed to the football field near the primary school and threw tennis balls for King for nearly an hour while he ran back and forth, chasing them and barking, having a wonderful time. The cold air nipped and woke me up, and the three of us played tag, laughing and jostling, helping to clear the horrible remnants from my mind. Then we threw more tennis balls for King, until we were all tired out.

"Euww," I said, picking up a ball. "Do you have to slobber on them?"

It's my gift to you.

"Just what I need – a sarcastic dog."

"Why do you say that?" Nicky said, but I couldn't answer

him. What could I say? That King talked to me?

Not a good idea.

No. I'd never hear the end of it. "He looks like he's sarcastic," I said. "You can see it in his face."

"He's very handsome," Nicky said. "And strong."

King sat and smiled, his tongue lolling out of his mouth.

I smiled back at him and then sighed. Maybe I was getting used to this dog talking thing. Or maybe I was already nuts. I said to Nicky, "Dad said we have to finish unpacking. So we'd better go home and get to work on it, I suppose."

As we ambled back to the house, my mood dived again into dark waters. I'd been putting off the last pile of boxes, hoping that we'd be out of Manna Creek within a week, when Dad realized what a crap town it was, and that we should go back to the city. But I could tell Dad was loving the place and his job already, even if Nicky and I were bored out of our brains. It would've helped if I'd seen some girls my own age around, but maybe it was too cold to hang around outside.

As if someone was granting me one small wish, a car drove past us and I spotted two girls in the back seat staring at us and King. One of them might've even been the same age as me. I could hope!

Dad walked through the backyard at lunchtime to grab a sandwich, and I asked him about the old building.

"Yep, it's one of the few original structures left in the town," he said. "Don't know how they'll restore it, but I've already had a woman in, telling me all about it and making sure we don't touch it."

"Who would want to?" I'd prefer to demolish it with a wrecker's crane.

"She thought we might pull it down if we didn't realize what it was."

"Nicky said there was a ghost in it." I tried to make it into a joke, ignoring a little fizz up my arms.

"If you believe in ghosts." He took a bite of his sandwich. "A man did die in there, she told me. Someone who came up here, looking for gold."

"How did he die?" Nicky asked.

"Er …" Dad glanced at Nicky's keen face. "He, um, hanged himself."

"Cool!" Nicky said.

"No, not cool at all," Dad snapped. "People dying is not entertainment, Nicholas, even if it was more than a hundred years ago."

"Sorry, Dad." Nicky blinked hard. He hated it when Dad growled at him.

"If you want to know about the history stuff, there's a little museum in the old church," Dad said. "Around behind the pub."

Yes, more top entertainment in Manna Creek. I couldn't wait.

"Time for me to get back to work," Dad said, slurping his coffee. "Sorry to leave you kids on your own so much, but it's full-on getting the station up and running, what with no one being here for more than six months."

I sat up straight. "I thought you said postings to one-man country police stations were really popular and hard to get," I said. "How come this one hadn't been filled?"

"I suppose it's because we're a fair way from Melbourne," Dad said.

"Like a million miles," I said. "We might as well be on the moon."

Dad's face drooped. "Don't you like it here?"

Nicky and I glanced at each other. "No, it's great, Dad," said Nicky.

"Yeah," I echoed. *Not.*

Dad brightened again. "That's good. And once you start school you'll make lots of new friends."

"Yeah," I said again. Why did everyone keep mentioning school? "Let's have a look in the museum, Nicky." It was better than nothing.

King was snoozing on the couch after his exercise, so Dad said we could go without him this time. "Just be careful and keep an eye out for any trouble." I nearly woke King up then, until a little doggy snore made me giggle.

Nicky and I headed towards the old pub, a mustard-colored, two-story building, with a happy hour advertisement painted on one of the windows. Someone had scratched off half the letters so it read *Hap Ho.* Around the back was the tiny museum, in a brick building with an empty bell tower on top.

"Is it open?" I said to Nicky. The building looked deserted – no lights were on – even though the sign on the door said the hours were 10 a.m. to 3 p.m.

He pushed at the wooden door, and it swung ajar. "Must be."

"Maybe we'd better – "

He disappeared inside without waiting for me, and I followed him slowly. The place smelled musty, like a charity shop, and it was freezing cold. I pulled my hat flaps down further over my ears and peered around. It was one large room, with a grimy, stained-glass window at the end and two dim light bulbs hanging on cords without shades. The walls were covered in ancient framed photographs and paintings, and a couple of glass cases sat in the middle of the room. Nicky was busy examining the photos.

"Here's that old police cell," he said. "It didn't look much better a hundred years ago." He brushed dust off the glass with his fingers.

I peered over his shoulder. "At least it had a roof then. Who's that standing in front of it?"

"Sergeant William Williams, 1st October 1894," Nicky read from the label.

"Our first policeman," someone behind me said. "A contributor to our fledgling community, for better or worse."

I spun around. A skinny old man blinked at me through thick glasses. His white shirt glowed in the dimness, and his hands shook as he inspected us.

"Who are you?" said Nicky.

"Jack Grimshaw," said the old man. "Just passing through, are you?"

"No, we live here now," I said.

"Ah, the policeman's children," he muttered. "Settling in all right, are you?"

I nodded politely. Nicky said, "There's a lot of history here."

"The museum, you mean?" He frowned. "Nobody bothers with it much these days, except me."

"What about the historical society?" Nicky asked.

"Just a group of nattering women," he said, scowling. "They barely set foot in here."

I glanced around again. No wonder nobody was interested. It was just a whole lot of old, dusty pictures. I pulled Nicky's sleeve. "Come on, let's go," I whispered.

"I want to look at the photos," he said.

Mr. Grimshaw glared at me and then beamed at Nicky. "There's a story behind every picture here, young fellow. Take a gander at this one." He tapped a photo on the wall next to him, and Nicky went over for a closer look.

Nicky was already pointing at things and asking Mr. Grimshaw questions before I stepped back through the doorway. The weak sunlight outside seemed bright and welcoming after the gloomy museum. Around the corner was the *Magical Moments* shop, and the woman – Tangine, I thought her name was – was sitting outside in a deck chair, reading a newspaper.

"Hello," she said, smiling. "Are you feeling better?"

"Yes, lots," I said. "My head feels foggy every now and then, that's all."

She got up from the chair. "I'm making tea. It's very nice and will help clear your head. Why don't you join me?"

"Oh. OK. Thanks." I felt awkward, remembering my refusal of the pendant, but I followed her into the shop, weaving my way between the piles of cushions and statues and beads to behind the counter. She pointed to a stool, and I sat down, watching as she plugged in a kettle and set out two blue-and-white striped cups and a matching teapot with a yellow sun on its lid. She didn't talk while she made the tea, so I glanced around at the things pinned to the walls. Horoscopes, astral signs, symbols and squiggly hieroglyphs, and a sign that said *Tarot Card Readings - $40*. I ignored that and looked at the postcards from all over the world and the photos of lots of different cats and dogs.

"Are they all yours?" I asked, waving at the cats and dogs.

"No." She laughed. "Well, that one was." She pointed at a regal-looking black cat sitting on a wall. "Wasabi."

"Wasabi's that hot green Japanese stuff, isn't it?"

"Yes, but the cat wasn't green, just grumpy." She poured boiling water into the teapot, then opened a tin decorated with Chinese paintings and put it in front of me. It contained chocolate cookies, and I took one, eating it while she poured two cups of vile-smelling tea. I looked at mine and wondered uneasily if it would be rude not to drink it.

"It's herb tea," she said, smiling at me. "It smells awful, but tastes good, and you need building up. Try it."

I held my breath and sipped. It wasn't as horrible as I expected – it tasted like dried grass with honey in it. Maybe I could drink some of it at least.

"How long have you lived here?" I asked her.

"About two years."

"Are you staying?" How did she make a living? Did anyone ever buy anything here?

She laughed. "For a while. Until the town no longer interests me."

"What's interesting in this dump?" I said.

"Many things. The people, the history, the bush."

"I guess the history stuff is in the museum."

"A little of it. Where's your brother?" She sipped her tea and pointed at mine, so I drank some more. She was right – my head was clearing.

"Nicky's in the museum, probably asking that Mr. Grimshaw a million questions."

"Mr. Grimshaw is a very interesting person," she said. "His family has lived in this area for more than a hundred years. They came here looking for gold, but never found any, so they stayed and farmed the land instead."

"So maybe his great-grandfather knew about the man who died in the old police cell?"

Her light blue eyes focused on me, and I felt like she was

lasering into my brain. "Mr. Grimshaw's great-grandfather *was* the man who died in the police cell."

"Oh. Sorry." Was it me, or were people around here ultra-touchy? I crossed my arms tightly and wished I'd never come into her shop. I looked away, pretending I was interested in a photo of a fox terrier, until she leaned forward and patted my hand.

"You weren't to know. He's a bit … obsessive about it."

I relaxed a little and let my arms drop. "Is that why he runs the museum?"

"Partly. But the history of the town is his passion." She poured herself more tea, but I shook my head when she offered it to me. "Mr. Grimshaw's family have never believed that their ancestor killed himself. They're sure that the policeman at the time murdered him."

"Who, Sergeant Williams?" When she raised her eyebrows, I added, "I saw the photo of him standing in front of the old cell. Are they right?"

"Who knows? But when someone believes a thing to be true, they won't listen to anything that says otherwise. And they carry their belief all the time, like a burden, or a debt."

I remembered the sergeant's cold, stern face and Mr. Grimshaw's glare, and shivered. "How do you know all this stuff?"

"I listen to people's stories," she said seriously.

"So you'd have heard about the sheep's head on our doorstep." Too late, I remembered that Dad had told me to keep quiet about it.

"It wasn't Mr. Grimshaw who did that," she said, and her eyes slid away.

"Who did?" And how did she know about it? Dad said no one knew except us. A worm of dread coiled through my stomach.

"It's not important – probably just a joke," she said, standing up and taking our cups to the small sink under the window.

"But, if you know, then –"

"I'm afraid you'll have to go. I have errands to run."

Her face was flushed, and she'd turned off her charm again, like a faucet. Anger rushed through me – that sheep's head had frightened me half to death! And here she was, refusing to tell me who did it. I jumped up from my stool, ready to demand she go and talk to Dad, but she was stony-faced, and before I knew it, my feet were moving to the door. I fought an urge to run. "Yeah, see you," I said over my shoulder.

I barged out of the shop, banging the door shut, and headed for the museum. The back of my neck prickled, but I refused to look around to see if she was watching me. What had I sensed in her shop? Danger? From what?

The museum doors were locked, and although I pounded hard with my fists, nobody came to open them. Nicky was nowhere in sight.

Was this the danger I'd felt? Not Tangine, but Nicky?

I needed to stay calm, to take some deep breaths and just chill out for once. But too many images were crowding into my head, banging against each other, making my skull feel like a battleground. The sheep's head, the rock, hitting my head, the old police cell, Tangine's face. And Dad's voice, saying, "You'd better stick together from now on."

Where was Nicky? Had he wandered off? I started running, faster and faster. I needed to know where he was. I needed to know he was safe.

Chapter Seven

I ran all the way back to our house, my heart pounding in my ears as my feet thumped along the sidewalk. My head ached and my lungs were bursting, but I didn't dare stop, and I rushed in through the front door.

"Nicky? Nicky!"

Silence.

I screamed, "Nicky!" again, then I heard his voice in the backyard. I raced through the kitchen and across the lawn to the steel shed, but Dad had locked it. I rattled the padlock. Where was he? "Nicky?"

"Here."

As I turned, sharp pain stabbed up under my ribs, and I

doubled over, holding my sides. I took deep breaths, tried to straighten, leaning against the shed, and scanned the yard. My vision blurred, streaked with red. "Where are you?" I gasped.

"In the old cell." He stood in the crooked doorway, framed by dried ivy and rotten wood. "What's wrong? Are you OK? Do you want me to call Dad?" His face was screwed up as if he was trying not to cry.

"No, I'm just …" I took another breath to calm down; I didn't want to scare him. "I was running. I've got a stitch, that's all." The pain in my stomach faded, and I managed to stand upright, but sweat trickled down my back. I forced my face muscles into a smile. "What are you doing in there? The historical ladies will have a fit."

"I wanted to look for myself. Mr. Grimshaw told me all about the man who died. It was his great-grandfather!" Nicky rubbed his hands on his jeans. "There's stuff in here still."

"Like what?" I wanted to drag Nicky away from the ramshackle cell, but I couldn't move.

"A rusted old bucket, a chair – but that's broken. And big iron rings in the walls. That's what they must've tied prisoners to. Come and look." He disappeared back into the cell and panic bubbled up again. Something foul was in there: something that made my whole body seize up. He shouldn't be in there!

"Aahhh!"

"Nicky, what's wrong?" His scream jolted me forward, breaking the spell; I ran across the lawn, barely noticing that

82

my skin had goose bumps from skull to toe. "Nicky?"

"Help me! I'm stuck," he said.

I stood in the doorway, trembling, trying to convince myself to go inside. My fear was a net, holding me back, but something else was piercing the net, drawing me in. It wasn't Nicky. He was in the furthest corner, half-crouching. "What's wrong?" I cried. "Stuck on what?"

"It's a big blackberry bush, growing through the gap on this side. It's hooked me right through my jeans, and the thorns are in my leg. You'll have to help me get it off."

"Is that all?" What else had I thought? Relief gushed through me, and I stepped towards him. Instantly, the cell darkened, and I could barely see. "What happened? Why is it so dark?" My goose bumps turned to tiny crawling feet. I shuddered and stepped back.

Nicky sniffed. "It's not that dark. Come and help me. Hurry up."

"Wait a minute," I said, blinking hard, gritting my teeth. I stepped forward, shaking, arms outstretched, and found him with both hands. As I touched him, the darkness lifted a bit, and I ran my fingers down to his legs to work out where the blackberry vine was. "Ow!" A thorn ripped into my thumb. I sucked it for a moment, but the stinging was hot and angry. Again, I tried to get a grip on the vine without its thorns attacking me, and this time I found a smoother bit. "Move back this way, Nicky – you're pulling on it and making it bite more."

He did as I told him, and after a few long moments I managed to unhook him. "There." I straightened and helped him up, brushing a tear from his face.

"Thanks, Sash. It still hurts. I hope blackberries aren't poisonous."

A low moan filled the cell, and the crawly feet skittered over my skin. "Don't make that dumb noise," I snapped. "It's not funny."

"What noise?" Nicky said.

The moan came again, louder this time, and I realized it wasn't coming from Nicky – it was behind me, or above. The roof – it was about to fall in. We had to get out! I grabbed Nicky's hand and spun around, then stopped as my sight suddenly cleared. I gasped, and my stomach lurched upwards.

On the floor in the opposite corner, a man sprawled, one arm up, his wrist shackled to a ring in the wall. His long black hair was matted and filthy; his clothes were as bad. But it was his face that was the worst – bloated red and purple, one eye swollen and closed, blood dribbling down from his nose and a cut above his eye. His breathing filled the cell, ragged and fast, tinged with a gurgle. My throat closed, and I stopped breathing. Somehow I knew he was almost dead, and there was nothing I could do. My muscles were desperate to move, but my brain screamed *No!*

"Sasha, you're hurting me," Nicky said, pulling his hand out of my grip.

"What?" I sucked in an abrupt breath and nearly choked.

I couldn't take my eyes off the man, and now I could smell him, too, as if he was going rotten as he lay there. Rotten like bad meat. I gagged, wrapped my hand over my mouth and nose.

"Don't you think this is cool?" Nicky said cheerfully. "No wonder they want to restore it." He poked at the rough stone blocks.

"Nick … can you see anyone else here?"

"No, 'course not." He peered at me. "What's wrong?"

"You can't smell anything?" The man moaned again, and then he turned his head and stared straight at me. His slitted eye was a sliver of red. I whimpered, but the sound stuck in my throat.

"No." He tugged at my sleeve. "Sash? What's happening? You look like you're about to toss your cookies."

"What?" The stupid phrase broke into the screaming fear inside my head, and at last I could turn away from the man. "What did you say?"

He shrugged. "It was on a video game I played. You look like a zombie." His face lit up. "Did you see a ghost?"

My eyes swiveled back to the corner. The man was gone. My guts swooped and dived. "No. Let's go." I grabbed his arm and half-dragged him out of the cell and across the lawn, ignoring his protests.

"King's barking like mad," Nicky said. "Maybe we should've let him out."

Inside the house, King was by the back door, hackles up.

He barked once, short and sharp. *What happened?*

You don't want to know.

Yes, I do. You disappeared.

I was in that horrible cell out there.

No, you disappeared. It felt like you no longer existed. Snuffed out.

A shudder rippled down my spine. "I saw a man in there."

"You did?" Nicky was agog, his eyes wide. "You really saw the ghost? Wow!"

"I don't know. I …" I retched and ran for the kitchen sink, heaving until my throat was raw, but only yellow dribble came up. Again, the retching made me feel better, as if I had expelled something more than just fluid.

"What did he look like? Did he look like Mr. Grimshaw?"

"Huh?" I shook my head, clinging to the edge of the sink. "I don't know. He … he didn't look like anyone. His face was all beaten up." King stayed out of my head, but I could feel his warm, calm presence, and it helped, like hugging my teddy bear when I was small.

"Wow. Wait till I tell Mr. Grimshaw," Nicky said.

"No!" I grabbed his arms and shook him. "You mustn't tell anyone, and especially not him."

"But –"

"Nobody, Nicky. Promise!" *They'll think I'm crazy.*

The look on my face must have convinced him. "OK." He hesitated. "Not even Dad?"

"No. Not yet." I felt the blood leech from my face. Dad

mustn't know this was happening to me.

You should tell him.

No.

I mustered up a smile for Nicky. "I will ... but Dad'll just say I imagined it anyway. Or that it was because I hit my head. He probably wouldn't believe me."

"But it's true, isn't it?" Nicky hugged me hard, and his nose dug into my chest. "I know you really saw him. You were freaking out, big time."

"Yeah, well ... I won't be going in there again, don't worry. And you shouldn't either." What if Nicky saw the thing? I couldn't bear it if he started having my nightmares.

"But it's so cool," he said. "Ghosts can't harm you." His grin faded. "Can they?"

"Something very wrong happened in there," I said, "and it's still there. Please, Nicky, don't go in alone."

He nodded, but I wasn't a hundred percent sure he meant it. His face still showed that glimmer of curiosity that he couldn't quite wipe away, and his chin jutted out stubbornly. I'd have to keep an eye on him for the next few days and make sure he stayed out of the cell. He opened the fridge and made himself a cheese sandwich while I boiled the kettle for hot chocolate. I added extra sugar to mine, wanting lots of sweetness to take away the awful taste in my mouth.

King sat next to me, his nose touching my leg every now and then.

What did you see?

I couldn't form the words in my head for him, but a picture of the man rose up in my brain.

King's neck fur stiffened. *Dangerous. Stay away.*

I know that already. What is it?

No idea.

That pulled me up. If I could talk to King in my head, why wasn't he aware of other stuff, like this ghost?

I'm a dog, not a psychic. I sense dog things and other stuff because of my training.

Right.

So I was alone with it, then. Like always. My stomach twisted again, and King nudged my leg.

You're not alone. Just because I can't see it doesn't mean I can't stay beside you and help. I know there's something bad there. You didn't imagine it.

Thanks. My throat ached, and I bent to give him a hug, rubbing my fingers through his soft chest fur. Then I made him a slice of buttered toast and myself a double-decker cheese and tomato sandwich, hoping that would settle my stomach, and it did. But I still wished that somewhere there was a person I could talk to about this stuff, someone who would understand and help me.

I had promised to be good for Dad, *good* meaning normal and well-behaved, like I used to be before Mum left. I felt I owed it to Dad; when I'd seen the disappointment and shame in his eyes after the court hearing, even though I'd been let off with a warning, I'd vowed to myself that I'd make him proud again. OK, I hated Manna Creek, but that paled next to trying to deal with all these weird things happening to me. Even Mum taking off was starting to seem less important.

I tried to think it all through – my head, King, seeing the ghost – but Nicky's Xbox was so loud, with its gunfire and sound effects, that I felt like my brain was going to explode. Outside, the sun was going down and it had clouded over, but I needed to get out of the house.

I'll come, too.

I went into the family room. "Nicky, I'm going out for a walk," I said. "I'm taking King, so you keep the doors locked. Promise?"

"I'll be OK. I saw Dad come back to the station before." He waved one hand at me, his eyes glued to the screen.

Should I tell Dad about Tangine? No, it seemed silly now, not worth worrying about. Dad was probably figuring it out already.

King and I walked up our street and stopped at the corner as I tried to clear my head and decide where to go. Then I turned towards the waterfall trail and quickened my pace.

Are you sure?

I want to look at where I think it started.

King trotted next to me, his ears forward, alert. There were a few cars in the main street, but people were all inside the shops. I turned down the trail, and immediately the world under the tree canopy grew darker. My feet stumbled on the uneven ground, so I concentrated on the trail ahead. I couldn't afford to fall again. Gum trees grew straight up to the sky, with leaf and twig debris underneath. The waterfall made a shushing sound that grew louder as we approached, and in a couple of minutes I was in the clearing by the weir. The trail along the creek was rougher and still slippery with damp leaves; in a few seconds we'd reached the place where I'd fallen. The fern between the trail and the creek was crushed, and there were still big boot prints in the soft earth.

I squatted and stared down at the water, deciding that the light-colored rock near the bank was the one my head had connected with. It was under the surface, which meant my head had been, too. Nicky was right when he said he'd saved me by pulling me out. I hugged my knees, and the stitches in the back of my scalp tightened.

I could've died, but instead, strange things started happening.
Are you sure?

"What do you mean?" I said it aloud, wanting to hear my own voice, hear myself talking about it sensibly.

You've been thinking about how you got sick in the backyard the first day you arrived. And talking to me has nothing to do with hitting your head.

"Hasn't it?"

No. I told you, you know how to listen to me, and you've probably had that gift all your life. You said when we met that you'd never had a pet.

We weren't allowed.

I stood up and walked back to the waterfall. An old

wooden bench sat to one side, and I sank onto it, thinking, remembering. First, it was a trickle of memory, then it all rushed in on me. What happened six years ago. How could I have forgotten?

You blocked it out.

Yes, I did.

When I was seven, the lady next door had a cat that followed me everywhere. One day, it kept jumping on and off me and making a lot of noise, meowing and growling, running back to its house and then into my room. In the end, I told Mum. She thought I was being silly at first, then she saw the cat doing it to me again, so she looked in the neighbor's window. She was lying on the floor, unconscious.

We all thought it was the cat being clever.

Then a few weeks later, Grandma came into my room one night after Mum had turned the light out. She gave me a big hug and said goodbye and told me to be good for Mum. The next morning I asked Mum if Grandma was going on a holiday, and told her what had happened. Mum laughed and said I'd had a nice dream, but about an hour later, the phone rang. It was Mum's sister telling her that Grandma had died. Grandma lived up in Sydney.

Remembering all this stuff was awful, like a thousand pins were piercing my brain and pricking into my skin. King jumped up on the bench beside me, and I put my arm around him.

"Why didn't the cat talk to me like you do?"

I think ... He touched my ear with his damp nose. *I think this is some kind of special bond. Animals will respond to you, but it seems that only you and I can talk.*

I hugged him. "That's a good thing. The best."

What else do you remember?

The prickling was back, even worse. "The man."

What man?

Again, talking helped me get it out of my head more clearly. "He got hit by a bus. I saw it on my way to school. It was horrible. He flew through the air, and I heard his bones crunch when he hit the ground." I grabbed King harder, burying my face in his throat fur, but I could tell he didn't mind.

"But then he disappeared, and the bus kept going like nothing had happened. I remember I threw up behind the bus shelter, and then I ran home because I felt so ill. I told Mum and insisted she find out if anyone had been killed by a bus, and she got upset with me. Said I had too much imagination. I had nightmares all night."

But?

"The next day I saw the man again. He was going to cross the road. He was reading a letter or something and not looking. I ran as fast as I could, and I stopped him just as he stepped off the sidewalk." My throat ached like I'd swallowed a sharp rock. "Then the bus zoomed past."

You saved him.

"I didn't know what was going on. I thought I had to be

there every day, for ever and ever, to save people. I couldn't tell Mum. I was scared she'd yell at me again. I had lots more nightmares. Mum was going to send me to see someone. A psychiatrist, I think."

So you blocked it all out.

"I guess so." I nodded. "I was desperate. I can still remember those nightmares, you know. I put up these pictures of kittens and bunnies on my wall next to my bed, and I stared at them for hours. Maybe my little kid's brain couldn't take any more because after a couple of weeks, it all kind of went away. And I eventually just stopped thinking about it."

Until now.

I straightened, my hand going to my mouth. "Oh, no, you're right."

About what?

"It *is* all the same thing, and it's come back. Why couldn't I see that's what was happening?" I jumped to my feet, wanting to run, run anywhere, get away from the sudden blaze of insight. But I couldn't. I was doomed. "My eyes blurring, the red at the edges. That's what it was like with the man and the bus. It's all starting again."

My mind was shouting *No*, and the memories of Grandma and the bus and the man flying through the air whirled around and around. I stood frozen, desperate to flee, but knowing in my heart that there was nowhere to escape to. It was all inside me.

But I didn't want it. I didn't! I had to make it go away again.

King growled, sitting up and sniffing the air.

Someone's coming, someone we don't want to find us here. Hide.

Chapter Eight

King and I ran to hide and dived into a small hollow behind some scraggly bushes. I raised my head slowly, peering through the bracken.

Stay completely still.

Scuffling footsteps and an out-of-tune whistling, then the person came into view. It was the greasy-haired man, wearing a dark gray beanie and a long black coat. He was carrying a backpack, and he stopped at the side of the clearing, scanning ahead before crossing open ground and moving along the trail towards town. When he was out of sight, I breathed freely again.

He gives me the creeps.

He's been up to no good.

Doing what?

Harvesting his little plantation.

"What? Does Dad know?" I stared at King. "How did you know?"

I can smell it. I didn't train as a drug dog, but you get to know the smell along the way. Your father hasn't found where the plants are yet.

Should I tell him?

No point. It won't be near here. He'll find it soon.

Let's go. It's nearly dark.

All the way home, my mind kept zinging back to my … I didn't know what to call it. My craziness? My brain meltdown? Every time I thought the word *gift*, I veered away from it as if it might mark me with a devil's fork or something. That was the kind of word Mum would use; it was like the rubbish you saw on TV, fake omens and spells and seeing dead people.

Isn't that what you do, though? King's eyes were on me, concerned.

Just let me think about it. On my own.

We walked in silence and made it home without seeing the greasy-haired man. Soon after, Dad came in from the police station. "What'll we have for dinner?" he said.

"Fish and chips," Nicky said.

"How about this?" Dad produced a large meat pie from of a plastic shopping bag and sniffed at it. "Smells great."

"Where did you buy that?" Nicky asked.

"Cass Sullivan brought it in for us."

"Isn't that what you call a bribe?" I said, grinning. "What's she done?"

"Nothing. She was just being friendly," Dad said.

"Is she married?"

"Sasha! She ... well, I'm not sure. I think she might be divorced." Dad's face was bright pink.

"Aha!" Nicky said. "You'd better look out then."

We all burst out laughing, but Dad looked a bit edgy, as if Nicky had come up with a very real possibility. Poor Dad. He still wasn't over Mum, even though she'd filed for divorce, which left him with no hope at all. I wished he'd forget all about her like I was trying to.

I filled King's bowl with extra dry food, changed his water and then made him some toast and peanut butter. He nudged my leg with his nose in thanks, then munched his way through the whole lot and settled down by the heater for the night. But I could tell he wasn't asleep – every now and then his eyes would open, and he'd regard us all for a few seconds. It was nice, like he was watching over us.

When I went to my room later, he lay on the rug next to my bed. I didn't feel like talking because I had more thinking to do. Did King know everything that went through my head? What if I met a boy I liked? Would he know what I was thinking about that kind of thing?

No, thank you. I'll stick to the basics.

I laughed and scratched his head, and he made a funny groaning noise.

You can keep that up for a week or two.

Eventually I lay down, and right away my brain skipped back to when I was little. I couldn't remember being hit on the head back then. But if I'd started doing this stuff when I was seven, did that mean it was inherited? I'd never heard of anyone else in our family acting weird, seeing things, but we didn't have much contact with our relatives. A lot of Dad's family lived overseas, some in New Zealand, some in Ireland. Mum only had one sister in Sydney that she hardly saw after Grandma died. Did it come from Grandma? Was her visit to me a way of passing it on as she died?

But I didn't remember feeling anything other than being happy to see her. It wasn't like she'd reached out a hand and blessed me – or cursed me, more like. It was so frustrating, not knowing or understanding. I wanted to punch something, or yell and scream. But that was pointless, so instead I dug out my favorite red nail polish and painted my nails, an activity that always calmed me down. I had to concentrate really hard to keep the polish even and smooth.

Inevitably, I went back to thinking about the gift again, and all the bizarre pieces of the puzzle made my brain spin, but I needed to sort it through; otherwise, I'd never sleep. If hitting my head on the rock had set it off again, could I stop it somehow? Hit my head again? No, too risky and painful. Force it away? Why had it disappeared when I was little?

Maybe it stopped once I saved that man. Dad often said there were reasons for things happening, even if we don't know all the facts at the time. I hated the idea that I was going to spend the rest of my life being haunted by ghosts and seeing horrible things like the man in the cell. I shuddered, remembering his swollen, bloody face.

King laid his muzzle on the side of my bed. *You don't mind being able to talk to me, do you?*

No, you're the good part.

He rolled over, his tongue hanging out. *I'm cute, aren't I?*

Yes, very cute. I giggled. *Are you looking for a girlfriend?*

Not around here. Not keen on sheepdogs and cattle dogs. Bit common.

Oh, I see.

Who could help me with this gift or curse? Tangine at the magic shop? No, despite the magic tricks and mystical tarot stuff, I didn't think she'd know anything about my problem. And she seemed pushy sometimes, like when she tried to force the pendant onto me, then she'd be all nice again. And then virtually shove me out the door.

Something else is bothering you.

You mean, other than seeing a half-dead guy who actually is dead?

Something from your own life.

King's quiet presence gave me courage, and I laid my hand on his head, traveling back to being seven again, allowing myself to try to recall every single thing about that episode with Grandma. Was there anything I'd missed? She hadn't been scary at all; I'd believed she really was in my room. But it was Mum's face after the phone call that had freaked me out. She looked at me as if I was evil, as if I frightened her, and she didn't know what to do with me. She didn't try to understand or help – her reaction was to act like I was contaminated. It hadn't sunk in then, not in a way I could describe at seven, but I'd known something was very wrong, and it was me who caused it.

I never told her about saving the man from the bus; I was terrified she'd send me away, or put me in the hospital, believing I was diseased. She focused instead on the nightmares, said they were just a passing phase, and I had to try harder to get over them. Had Grandma had a gift? Had Mum known about it? No one had ever mentioned it. A sudden new insight jerked me upright. Maybe Mum had known, and she was either terrified of it, or wanted to crush it out of me. Why hadn't she helped me?

Anger flared inside me. It wasn't my usual anger about Mum deserting us – she could stay on the Gold Coast with her stupid boyfriend in his black sports car forever – I didn't miss her a bit. No, this anger was about the way she'd deserted me back then, treating me like I had the plague, getting grumpy about being woken by my screaming when I was having nightmares every night.

Many humans are afraid of what they don't understand.
She was my mum!

True.

King ruffed deep in his throat and moved right in close to rest his muzzle on my arm. His warm breath tickled my skin.

I thought you only listened to the basics.

This is important to you.

I stared up at the cracked ceiling. *What am I going to do? I feel like a total freak, like one of those outcasts in India that everyone will reject and throw out.*

Stop trying to fix it. And anyway, who needs to know? Wait and see what happens. You humans need to learn more patience.

It might drive me crazy.

You're stronger than you think.

Tears slid down the sides of my face. I didn't feel strong, I felt incredibly alone, and the only one who understood, who I could talk to, was a *dog*. Would I ever be able to tell Dad about this? Desolation washed through me, and I clung to what King had said. *Wait and see what happens.* Maybe the gift would go away again and leave me in peace.

King didn't bother to reply, just licked my arm comfortingly. My last thought before I dropped off to sleep was, *It'd be nice to see Grandma again.*

Later, I couldn't decide if the dream had been a dream the whole time, or if I'd woken up halfway through and "seen" the rest of it. It hardly mattered.

I was in Mrs. Alsopp's old white house, walking through

all the rooms, touching her things, picking them up to look at them and carefully putting them down again. I inspected all of her paintings, too, even the dark, dreary ones of forests and wagons of hay. It was really hot in her house, and I kept wanting to tell her to stop putting wood in the stove, but I couldn't find her.

I turned the corner near the kitchen and stopped to look at a painting I hadn't seen before. It looked like a Nolan, one of his Ned Kelly paintings with the square black helmet. My legs were so hot, and when I looked down, there were flames creeping along the floor, growing bigger by the second, and then rushing up the walls, as if the wind was pushing them.

I tried to get through to the kitchen. I knew she was in there, making me a cup of tea, but the flames were too high. I had to get out before I died, but something made me decide to grab the Nolan painting. When I turned back to the wall, it had disappeared, and I screamed because the flames were licking up my legs.

"Sasha! Sasha! Wake up."

My eyes were already open, I knew that, but I couldn't see anything except the flames. Then gradually I focused on Dad, his anxious face, and Nicky and King. They were all staring at me. Dad shook me again and then cupped my face in his hands.

"Are you OK?" Dad asked. "You were having a nightmare but … your eyes were open."

"You looked like a zombie," Nicky said.

What did you see?

I sat up, pulling back from Dad, and stared at King. "Mrs. Alsopp. Her house is on fire." I dug my fingers into Dad's hand. "You have to call the fire department. Hurry! She'll die!"

"It was a dream, love," he said. "She would've called if there was a fire."

"No, she can't. She's lying on the kitchen floor. She might be dying." I could hear my voice getting more and more hysterical, but the vision of the old lady and the flames was so vivid that I knew it wasn't a dream – and it wasn't something that was going to happen tomorrow. It was happening right now. "Dad, you have to do something! Please!"

"All right." Dad rubbed his jaw. "I'll call Jack from the Volunteer Firefighters – he lives further up the hill – but I won't be popular. It's nearly midnight."

"Just do it. Hurry."

He went off to fetch his mobile phone, and I could hear him in the next room, muttering into it. I listened intently, dread coating me like an oil slick, and caught phrases – "Sorry to wake you ..." and "Could you have a look?" Then, "Right, OK. Yes. I'm on my way."

He didn't come back into my bedroom. Instead, we heard him pulling clothes out of drawers, keys jangling as he collected his gear, ready to move out. At the last minute, he put his head around my door.

"You two, stay here and lock the doors. I'll call you when I know something." He focused on me for one long second.

"I'll talk to you later."

The front door slammed and the 4 x 4 started up, then roared away. I'd started shivering and pulled a sweatshirt out of my drawer and put it on.

Nicky was goggle-eyed. "Is her house really on fire?"

"Um … I think so." I didn't know how much to tell him. *Not much.*

"Is this like the ghost in the cell?" he said. He was shivering, too, standing at the end of my bed, and I wasn't sure if it was cold or fright. Could I trust him to understand? I just knew I didn't want to see the same expression on his face that I'd seen on Mum's. Like I was evil.

"No, it was a dream. I didn't, well … I don't know, Nicky." I beckoned to him. "Come here, kiddo. You want to get into bed with me?"

He resisted for a moment, probably thinking he was too big for cuddles, then he caved in. "OK." He snuggled in next to me, and I tucked the tiger under his arm. King lay down again.

"Did you – " Nicky began.

"Go to sleep. Dad won't be back for ages. We'll find out all about it in the morning."

He was asleep in a few minutes, but I knew I'd be wide awake until dawn, until there was enough natural light back in the world to make me feel a little safer.

Chapter Nine

Dad didn't come home for breakfast, and he didn't call. The house seemed even smaller and drabber than normal, and King followed us from room to room. Nicky and I ate our cereal with the TV on, not because we wanted to watch cartoons, but because we wanted some noise instead of the thick silence. When the phone rang, we both jumped, and I ran to answer it.

It was Dad. "I won't be home for a while yet." His voice was loud against some shouting in the background and the buzzing of a chainsaw. "I've got to set this up as a crime scene and wait for the boys from Melbourne to arrive."

"A crime scene?" I said, clutching the phone. My legs felt

boneless, and I sat down fast. "What happened?"

"It's not good news, Sash. Mrs. Alsopp is dead, I'm afraid."

"Oh." The rock in my stomach doubled in size, and I sagged under its weight. "That's awful."

"They've saved a lot of the house, but it was too late for her. I'm sorry. I wish we could've saved her."

"But what happened? How did the fire start? You said it was a crime scene …"

Someone shouted closer to Dad, calling his name. "I'm really sorry. I have to go, Sasha." His deep voice resonated with kindness, but the word *dead* tolled like a bell in my head. "Look after Nicky, and stay out of trouble."

"Right. Bye." I pressed the button and sat staring at the phone. A crime scene meant that the fire had not been an accident or an electrical fault. My heart felt like it was being squeezed – I should have known she was in danger!

"Why are you crying?" Nicky asked.

"Huh?" I hadn't realized, but tears were dripping down my face. I let them fall. "That nice old lady we met, the one who gave us cookies. She's dead."

Nicky's mouth dropped open. "And you dreamed it."

"I did not!" But I had. Just not soon enough to save her. Inside my chest, hot fingers seized my lungs so hard I couldn't breathe. That's what freaked me out about this stuff – was I supposed to save people? If so, I was doing a really bad job. The tissues were on top of the fridge; as I reached for them, I saw Nicky's face. His mouth was scrunched up, and his chin trembled as he tried hard not to cry. My own misery dropped away as I rushed to give him a big hug.

"Hey, don't worry, Nicky. It'll be OK. Accidents like this happen. It's nobody's fault." The lie boomed like a bass drum in my head, but I couldn't tell him the truth. Not right now. I rubbed my face with my sleeve and said, "Come on. I'm sick of this depressing house. Let's finish unpacking our gear and put all our pictures up. Make it bright and cheery, just like home, I mean, Melbourne."

"Uh … all right."

Nicky probably wanted to spend the morning on his Xbox, but I wasn't going to let him. The noise would drive me nuts, and we both needed to be busy. A part of me still couldn't accept we were here for the long-term, but surrounding ourselves with our favorite things would help all of us feel better, as well as more normal. I managed to venture out to the shed and bring in our boxes without the old cell affecting me too much. I refused to even look at it, keeping my eyes on my shoes. *Mind over matter, mind over matter*, I kept telling myself. Ignore it and it will go away, like it did before.

As well as unpacking, we cleaned and vacuumed, and I sprayed vanilla air freshener everywhere, making King sneeze. By lunchtime, the house looked a little more like home and less like a tattered brown and gray box. I helped Nicky put up all his football posters, and I pinned up art prints that I'd had for ages, stored away in tubes.

"What're those meant to be?" Nicky asked.

I surveyed the prints arranged along the wall by my bed. They were definitely not pictures of kittens and bunnies. "That one is *The Maiden* by Gustav Klimt, and the other one is part of one of Monet's waterlily paintings. And this," I pointed to a smaller picture of a sculpture, "is *The Thinker* by Auguste Rodin."

Nicky peered at *The Thinker*. "Why is he thinking with no clothes on?"

I laughed. "Rodin was fantastic at bronze sculptures of the human body. I guess he thought it was more interesting to show the muscles."

"So how come *you* don't draw and paint anymore?" Nicky said.

My mouth went dry, and I tried to shrug like it didn't matter. "I don't know. I kind of stopped for a while, and … other things happened." I bit my lip, unable to meet Nicky's eyes. I gazed at *The Maiden* instead, loving all over again the patterns and spirals of color, the perfect faces. I'd gone through a stage of imitating Klimt's style, spending hours on patterns of my own. I remembered the feel of the pen in my hand, my stiff neck when I finally looked up …

Nicky touched my hand, his small fingers cool. "I heard Mum and Dad talking once, and they said you were really talented. That you should go to art school."

"I'm not good enough for that," I said automatically.

"How do you know if you don't actually do it?"

His words cut through, slicing into a part of me I thought I'd gotten rid of. The part called hope.

It all came back to Mum again. She'd always raved about my art, bought me brushes and paints and charcoal, entered my work in local competitions. After she'd left, I ripped up every single piece I'd ever drawn, and I burned the paintings that couldn't be ripped.

Dad had been devastated. "Oh, Sasha," he said, his mouth drooping down.

I'd pushed him away. "I don't care about that rubbish anymore. I never want to draw or paint again. And I don't want to talk about it." And I especially didn't want to talk about Mum, or think about her. Oh, I hated her!

And then not long after that, I'd started shoplifting and staying out late, hanging around with an older crowd. I'd even tried smoking, but it was disgusting, so I faked it, trying to look cool. I should've learned when I was caught stealing, but instead I went joyriding with two of the guys in a stolen car. Yeah, Mum was really cut up about that when Dad told her. Not. She didn't bother to call, even then. Not that I would've talked to her anyway.

"Sasha?" Nicky poked me. "You could do paintings a million times better than that awful man in the gallery. He could be selling *your* paintings, and you could make lots of money."

I snorted. "Yeah, sure, and pigs might fly, too. Get real, kiddo. That man would kick me out in five seconds."

Nicky examined each print again. "I like these. Let's go to the gallery and have another look at those expensive paintings you liked. Then you might change your mind."

"Not likely." But it was better than hanging around, waiting for Dad. Or thinking about Mrs. Alsopp. "OK, I would like to see the Boyd paintings again."

The gallery door was closed, but an *Open* sign hung in the window, so we tried the handle, which turned. Leaving King outside sitting next to a row of cacti in a sheltered porch area, we crept in and closed the door quietly. An elderly couple were wandering around, looking at the paintings and sculptures and murmuring together. Nicky hovered near them, obviously eavesdropping, and then came back to me, grinning.

"They don't like the fork and spoon thing either," he whispered. "The man called it derivative. What does that mean?"

"It's not an original idea, that someone else has already done it better."

"See, you know heaps about all this," he said, and went to look at the gallery owner's bizarre paintings again.

I focused on the four paintings on the far wall near the desk, the ones I thought were originals, wondering where the gallery man was, although it was a relief not to have him glaring at me. I stood in front of the Boyd paintings for ages, going from one to the other. Both of a familiar subject, the Shoalhaven River. Yes, that's how gum trees were around here,

I realized. Tall silver and white trunks, soaring upwards, all their leaves at the top. The paintings' frames were old, maybe secondhand, the gilt worn off in patches. One frame had a big chip out of the side of it, exposing bare wood underneath the varnish, leaving the scrolled bit half-finished. Why hadn't the paintings been reframed, if they were worth so much?

I peered closer, examining the brush strokes, the way the colors moved into each other, the layers and shades, wishing I could paint like that. Imagining a brush in my hand, the paint sliding across the canvas. But I didn't paint anymore. And never would again.

Except that my fingers were almost twitching, and I felt the familiar urge to grab a pad of art paper and a pencil and draw. It hadn't gone away. It was like the other thing: I'd squashed it down, out of sight, but now it was popping up again, out of control. Was I happy about it? My hand curled, shaping a brush. Yes. No. What was the matter with me?

Nothing. King's voice was faint, but clear.

Yeah, right.

The elderly woman and man had left – the only other thing in the room was the gray cat. Then I heard the gallery man's voice. He seemed to be shouting at someone on the phone.

"I don't care! It was a stupid thing to do … You don't know that … They'll have to wait … It's too close … No …" Then he slammed the phone down.

Even through the wall, I could sense his rage. Who was

he talking to? What was stupid? What was he up to? The way he was yelling freaked me out. I didn't want to be around when he came back into the gallery. "Let's go," I said to Nicky, pulling him with me.

For once, he didn't object, and we were outside again in a few seconds. My heart was pounding – I didn't like the gallery man, but it wasn't as if he'd been yelling at me. Still, what was he so angry about?

When we got back to the house, we found Dad in the kitchen; he sat, head in hands, with a cup of coffee in front of him. His face was smudged with dark streaks, and his hands were almost black.

"Hi. What've you two been doing?" he asked wearily.

"We've been at the gallery on the corner," Nicky said. "Sasha's going to –"

"No, I'm not," I interrupted. "Are you OK, Dad?"

"Yeah, just tired. And a bit upset about poor old Mrs. Alsopp."

The early certainty I'd felt about her death had been niggling at me all day. Was I right? "Why was the fire a crime scene? Wasn't it an accident?"

"No, it wasn't." Dad never told us all the gory details of his police work, but neither did he try to cover up things with fluffy words. "The fire investigator found evidence of an accelerant; it wasn't faulty wiring or her wood stove."

"And she couldn't get out in time?" I asked. "No smoke alarms?"

"There were, but she wouldn't have heard them. Someone knocked her unconscious."

"What?" *It was murder?* I felt as if someone had punched me in the throat, but Dad didn't notice.

He rubbed his eyes and went on, "The firemen got the fire under control before it burned the whole house down. It was pretty obvious someone helped themselves to a lot of her paintings, including a Sidney Nolan one of Ned Kelly." He glared at us. "And all of that information stays in this kitchen, right?"

Nicky nodded. "Who would we tell?"

I sat in shocked silence – I'd seen the Nolan painting in my dream!

"I'd bet my last dollar that you'll get questions from people around the town," Dad said. "The gossip networks will be running hot. But if I'm right, and a local is involved, I don't want any information getting out. The fire crew has already been told to keep their mouths shut."

"Are forensics here now?" I asked.

"Yes." Dad sighed. "I have to go back up there later this evening and guard the site for a few hours. The fire analysis guys are there as well as more police. It's all been taped off, but you know what it's like. People want to come and look."

"Dad …" I hesitated, the heavy fist on my chest now, making me short of breath. "Could you have saved her if you'd gotten to her house sooner?"

"No," Dad said shortly. "The fire produced a lot of smoke,

they said, which is what often kills people." He ruffled Nicky's hair, his expression grim, as if he was regretting telling us so much. "Let's have something to eat, shall we, Nicky? I need a decent meal instead of sandwiches." He glanced at me and shook his head slightly, as if to say he'd speak to me later.

He was going to ask about my dream. I rubbed my breastbone and tried to breathe normally, glad not to have to explain now. The last thing we needed was Nicky having nightmares, too. Dad made us steak and eggs, and then we all ate the last pieces of pound cake, wishing we had another one. "Maybe I'll have to ask for the recipe," I said.

"You can't cook!" Nicky said.

"I can learn," I said. "There's nothing else to do."

"You'll have plenty to keep you busy when school starts," Dad reminded me. "Only a few more days to go."

"Hmph." I wondered whether I should tell him about the gallery man, but what would I say? That he shouted on the phone? That he was nasty? No crime in that. I kept quiet as Dad changed his filthy clothes and crossed the backyard to the police station. Soon after, I looked out the window and saw the gallery man marching up the station path, all puffed up and red-faced. I left Nicky watching afternoon TV and crept past the shed, sticking close to its wall and away from the cell so my stomach didn't churn as badly. Dad had the back door of the station propped open, the trash can waiting to be put out, so I could eavesdrop easily.

"What are you doing about these burglaries?" The gallery

man's voice was raised, as usual.

"We're investigating every angle, Mr. Jones-Sutton," Dad said calmly. "Have you had something stolen from your gallery? I don't have any record of it."

"No, of course not. My security is excellent, and I live on the premises. But half of the paintings that've been stolen were bought from my gallery. It's making me look bad!"

"Er, I'm not with you," Dad said. "What do the burglaries have to do with you? That's like me getting my car stolen and blaming Toyota."

"Don't patronize me, man! My clientele are from the top echelons of society. They talk to each other, and if nothing else, they're going to think buying from me is bad luck. Or they might assume my artworks are being targeted, especially in this area."

"That's assuming a bit too much, I'd say." Dad cleared his throat, which I knew was his signal that he thought Mr. Jones-Sutton was being a bit of an idiot. "We have a team from Melbourne up here at the moment. If you have any information, you could talk to them."

"About what? A fire? What would I know about that?"

But he does know! It hit me like a slap. How did he have information about the fire and the robbery already? Nobody else in town knew paintings had been stolen. Had Dad picked up on this?

But Dad had changed direction. "Have you sold Mrs. Alsopp anything from your gallery?"

"No. She did ask me up to value some things a few months ago, but she wouldn't have bought any of my work. She barely had room for what she already owned."

"Did you happen to make a list of what she owned?" Dad asked. "It could be handy for us."

"Of course not! Most of it was worthless anyway."

"Hmmm. Well, thanks for coming in. Have a good day."

"But … but … what about the burglaries? What about my paintings?" I could imagine the gallery man was probably spitting all over the counter by now.

"I don't believe any of your paintings have been stolen."

"No, not mine … Oh, very well, but if you don't find this thief soon I'll be writing a letter of complaint to the Police Commissioner."

"You're welcome to do that," Dad said politely. After the door slammed, he muttered, "And stick your fat head in the envelope, too."

I decided it was time to say something. "Dad? It's me."

"Sasha – is something wrong?" Dad looked anxious as I walked into the main office.

"No, 'course not." I peered out through the front window. Mr. Jones-Sutton was nowhere in sight. "That man is horrible. And he knows about Mrs. Alsopp's paintings being stolen."

"How do you know that?" Dad looked astonished.

"He said so." Oops. Maybe he hadn't. Maybe I'd sensed it somehow. "Well, maybe he didn't, but you should've asked him about it."

"We're keeping that quiet for now," Dad said. "He's angry because he thinks people will stop buying paintings from him, that's all. He might even be right, but not for the reasons he gave. Bad luck, my foot!"

I ran Mr. Jones-Sutton's words back through my head, and my certainty grew. Maybe he hadn't said anything suspicious, but I still knew he was involved. "I think you should watch him. Maybe he's the thief. And he'd know what a Sidney Nolan was worth."

"Sasha, leave the police work to me, all right? And don't go accusing people when you have no evidence at all. That's the kind of thing that can set the whole community against us."

"Sorry. I just …" Had I gotten it wrong? I was so sure about Mr. Jones-Sutton – but was I making too much of that phone call? I sighed. Like Dad said, I had no real evidence, so I'd better keep my mouth shut.

"Now, I wanted to talk to you about the dream you had. You told me Mrs. Alsopp's house was on fire. How on earth did you know?"

Dad had his interrogation face on, the one that he used when we'd done something bad. I'd seen that before, and I'd hoped never to see it again. I couldn't lie to that face. It made me open my mouth and spill everything out, whatever Dad wanted to know. It was freaky, like my jawbone disconnected.

Right then, explaining my dream was the absolute last thing I wanted to do. If Dad looked at me the way Mum had, like I was abnormal or evil, my whole world would shatter like a glass bowl dropped on concrete. And so would I. My eyes veered wildly around the office and then zeroed in on the front door. I had to get out of there, no matter what.

"Later, Dad, OK? I need to go for a walk – my head aches, you know? Fresh air. That'll help." As I gabbled, I ran around the counter, raced to the door and pulled it open. "We'll talk later, promise." But if I had anything to do with it, we wouldn't.

I didn't look back and walked all the way around the block rather than cut through the backyard and pass the cell again. How long could I avoid Dad's questions? I felt guilty, even though I wasn't really lying to him, and his stern face made it ten times worse. A freezing wind blasted through the town, and I shivered, wishing I had worn my coat. Head down, arms wrapped around myself, I nearly walked straight into someone.

"Hey, watch where you're going, stupid!"

The voice wasn't familiar, but when I looked up and saw who it was, I instinctively stepped back, ready to run.

Chapter Ten

The big, dark-haired boy from the shop stood in front of me, his face twisted into a sneer. I struggled to remember his name – Mark, that was it, Mark Wallace. Standing by Mark's legs, head forward, teeth glinting, was the mangy yellow-and-brown dog I'd first seen as we drove into town. Its slitty eyes and small ears suggested pit bull in there somewhere. Dog and boy both looked hostile, like they wanted to rip someone to pieces. A low growl from the dog made me step back.

"H-hi," I said. "Sorry, I didn't see you."

"Sorry, I didn't see you," Mark mimicked, in a high voice. "Typical pig, think you own the sidewalk."

There was only one person that hated police being called

pigs more than Dad – me. A retort burst out of my mouth. "Can't you think of a better insult than that?"

"I'm not into words – I'm into action," he said, and the dog growled again. It wasn't on a leash, and its front feet were scrabbling slightly on the cement, as if it was getting ready to leap at me. "You wanna start something?"

"'Course not," I said, trying to sound tough, fighting the urge to make a run for it. "Bit of a waste, beating up a girl, isn't it?"

"Not if it's a girl pig." He leaned forward, as if he was going to spit on me, and I took two more shaky steps backward, my knees too wobbly to bend properly.

Right away, the dog stalked forward and growled again, but this time its matted neck fur stood up, too. I froze. There was no one in sight, and I was still too far from home or the police station to scream for help. Not that screaming would do me any good if the dog attacked me.

It'd go for my arms first, or maybe my face. I'd seen photos of people with their faces ripped apart by a dog's teeth. Fear gripped my body with steel fingers, but my brain kicked into overdrive. I tried desperately to think, plan, remember, visualize defense – anything at all!

What should I do with my hands? Cross my arms? Could I defend myself that way? I wanted to run, but the thought of the dog attacking me from behind was worse. What to do? As my brain skittered around, I latched onto one thing I knew – had Dad told me? – didn't matter. Stare at the ground, don't

look the dog in the eye. Concrete, weeds, wooden fence …
The grip loosened slightly. What about trying to get into its
head? If it worked with King, maybe it would work here, too.

Go away! Step back. Go away! Lie down.

No effect. I couldn't catch any kind of dog communication
from the animal at all, not even a beam of hate. But still it
growled and leaned towards me.

"Scared of my dog, are ya?" Mark folded his arms and
smirked. "One word from me, and you're history. Wanna
know what the word is?"

"No."

"Here's another word. Hold."

The dog closed in on me and put its heavy, muddy paw
on my foot. A whimper curdled in my throat, and an insane
voice in my head told me the dog was making my shoe dirty.

"See, that's what I tell him when we're hunting. He knows
the injured animal is trying to get away, and his job is to hold
it until I'm ready."

I shuddered and felt sweat trickle down my back under
my shirt. This kid was a lunatic, and if I tried anything, I
knew I'd come off worse. I had to wait it out, hope he'd get
bored with taunting me, and take his horrible dog home.

I swallowed hard. "He's well trained."

"Yeah. Me and Dad trained him together. You know my
dad, don't you?"

I shook my head, but a wire arced across in my head and
connected. Greasy-haired man. The dog looked different when

it was panting to kill someone.

"Well, he knows you." He laughed, a high-pitched whinny.

I'm coming.

King! I slumped with relief, and immediately the dog growled louder, and Mark's gaze sharpened. "Don't you try anything, Miss Piggy."

King came around the corner at a fast, steady pace up to where we were standing. He barked twice and stopped next to me. *Don't move.* The mangy dog took his paw off my foot and bared its teeth at King, growling so loud that I thought it was going to attack any second.

King stood, his head level, focused on the other dog. Even though King was almost twice its size, the mangy dog was vicious and ready to fight. It'd probably been trained to go for the throat, but it was also apparently trained not to move until told to. I hoped Mark had more sense.

"What's that thing?" he said.

"A German shepherd, actually." I hoped it was nervousness I heard in his voice. "Trained police dog. Belongs to us now." I held my breath.

Stay calm.

"I'd call it a pig dog," Mark said, his lip curling, "but that'd be putting dirt on all the good pig-hunting dogs around here."

"Off to do some hunting now, are you?" I said carefully.

His eyes flickered, and he glanced away, the first sign

of backing down, perhaps. *Oh, please, go.* "Yeah, Dad'll be waiting for me. No time to waste on pigs like you." He turned abruptly and walked off, whistling for his dog who whipped around and trotted after him – neither of them looked back.

I crumpled against the fence, unable to speak for a few moments, blinking back the tears that suddenly flooded my eyes.

Close call.

"Sure was. That kid is crazy." I knelt down and put my arms around King, ruffling his fur and feeling his heartbeat. "Thanks. I thought I was dead meat then. And another trip to the hospital. Dad would've loved that."

Tell him what happened.

"Don't worry, I will." As I stroked his ears, something occurred to me. "How come that dog couldn't hear me like you do?"

Most dogs and cats can't, or they don't want to.

"Oh. Is it a choice thing then?"

No, ability. That dog hates everybody. That's all it's filled with.

"It even hates its owners?"

Them most of all.

I shivered. The sweat had dried, and I was cold again. We walked home and sat in front of the heater until Dad came in, then I told him what had happened.

"You'd better steer clear of that family," Dad said. "I'm pretty sure it was the father who dumped the sheep's head and broke our window."

The connection sparked in my head again. "The Wallace family. Lovely."

Nicky had been listening. "There's lots of bad people in this town, Dad. Like the city."

"Not really," Dad said. "It's just that we live close to them, and this place is not very big. They tend to stick out more. Nowhere to hide."

"Nowhere for us to hide either," I said.

"King did a great job looking after you," Dad said. "Make sure you stick together and take him with you all the time, until I sort this Wallace family out. I need to pay them a visit, I think. I'm not putting up with this sort of behavior."

I wasn't sure Dad playing the heavy would help much, but I knew I couldn't ask him to ignore it. And I didn't want to.

I'll look after you both.

"How did King know you needed help?" Nicky asked me. "One minute he was asleep next to me, the next he was barking like crazy, trying to get out the front door. I didn't know what to do, but he kind of made me open the door, and then he took off."

"I ... um ..."

"He must've sensed something," Dad said, bending down to pat King's head. "Good dog."

Steak would be a nice thank you.

"Let's have steak tonight," I said, "and I think King deserves some, too." Plus, discussing whether we'd barbecue or grill it would take Nicky's mind off how King knew I was in

124

trouble. I could hardly say he'd *heard* me! But for once I was glad of the gift, glad that at least this part of it helped me for a change.

After dinner, Dad came into the family room holding something behind his back. He glanced at Nicky, who nodded eagerly. "Er, Sasha, I've got something for you. It's, um ... here." Dad handed me a pad of art paper and a bunch of pencils and charcoal sticks. "I kept them, just in case. Had them packed in one of my boxes."

"But ..." I twisted my fingers, entwined them. I wanted to say I didn't draw and paint anymore, that I'd meant what I said when I'd destroyed everything, but I knew it wasn't true. My hands had been itching all day, especially in the gallery, itching to pick up the charcoal or pencil and sketch something, anything. "I don't ..."

"Yes, you do," said Nicky. "I told Dad how your face was all glowing in the gallery and when you put your posters up. Go on, take them. And then you can draw a picture of me, like you used to."

Of their own accord, my hands reached out and took the pencils and charcoal, and I thrilled to the feel of them in my fingers. "Oh, yeah," I teased Nicky, "how did I know it would be about you?"

"I remember that picture you drew of Mum. It was so ..." Too late, Nicky realized that was a topic best left alone. He snapped his mouth shut, his face pink. Dad gave King another pat on the head.

"I'll draw a picture of you on one condition," I said quickly. "You have to sit still and not talk for thirty whole minutes. As soon as you open your mouth, I stop."

"Easy-peasy," Nicky said, smiling again.

As I expected, it wasn't easy at all. After ten minutes of sitting for me, Nicky started talking, and I had to shush him half a dozen times, but finally I had something that resembled him. I was pleased and disappointed at the same time – I'd grown rusty.

"That is so cool!" Nicky's face was bright with happiness as he held it up for a better look.

Dad peered over Nicky's shoulder. "Amazing, Sash. You really do have a gift."

"Yeah, well … maybe I'll do one of you tomorrow, eh, Dad? You can put it up in the station as a *Wanted* poster."

"Cheeky," Dad said, laughing.

But later, sitting up in bed with the pad and charcoal, what did I end up drawing but the ghost in the cell. The portrait just happened, flowing out of the stick onto the paper before I could stop it. Each sweep and stroke of the charcoal made me cringe in horror, but my hand kept moving, slashing and jabbing the last few lines. I captured everything, from his shackled wrists hanging down from the iron rings to his swollen face to his ragged trousers and worn-out boots, as if he was right in front of me.

As soon as I'd finished, I stared down at his face, my hands trembling. It was so ugly and revolting, like a scar that puckered my own skin and flared at me in the mirror every day. I wanted to screw the page up and throw it away. Was I going to be haunted by this man forever? Would I have nightmares about him? I wanted to reach in and rip him out of my brain.

And yet … I'd captured something else as well as his revolting injuries. Something that hinted at determination or stubbornness, a glimmer of inner strength that helped to settle my jumping nerves. Had I put it there myself? Or had I somehow seen it beyond his pain and suffering? Instead of destroying the drawing, I tucked it behind my chest of drawers. I wasn't sure why – maybe because I hadn't drawn for so long that I hated to destroy my first new efforts. As long as I didn't look at it again, I'd cope.

Except that the ghost filtered into my dreams. I was in Manna Creek, walking the streets, and every corner I turned, there he was, lying on the sidewalk. In his eyes was a pleading expression, and a couple of times I thought I heard him say, "Help." I woke up covered in sweat and shaking, and when I couldn't get back to sleep, I went out to the kitchen and made myself some hot chocolate. A light under his door showed Dad was still awake, but I didn't want to talk to him. King padded into the kitchen after me.

I saw what you were dreaming about. It was very clear. What does he want?

You tell me! I stirred the chocolate roughly, splashing it onto the counter.

127

He was still alive. Like when you saw him in the cell.

So?

But he was dying.

My spoon rattled against the side of the mug. *What am I supposed to do about it? That was over a hundred years ago.*

Think about the people you've seen. What did they have in common?

I shrugged. *I saw them … I don't know … not dead.*

But they were about to die, and you saved them.

Not Mrs. Alsopp.

No. King huffed. *That was an impossible situation, out of your control. But this ghost is different. You need to investigate it further.*

How?

Ask his descendant.

"What? Mr. Grimshaw?"

I'd spoken out loud, and Dad called, "Sasha? You all right?"

"I'm fine, Dad, just making a hot drink."

"OK."

Mr. Grimshaw's too grumpy to talk to.

Take Nicky with you. The old man likes his curiosity. It'll be a good cover for you.

I went back to bed after drinking my chocolate, and with King on the floor next to me, I managed to fall asleep again. This time there were no nightmares, and I slept in until nearly 9 a.m. Nicky had already eaten and was back on his Xbox.

"Aren't you sick of that thing?" I said, as I ate some muesli.

"Nup. I swap games if I get bored."

"Want to go and see Mr. Grimshaw this morning?"

"Sure." He glanced at me. "Are you going to tell him about the ghost?"

"No! And don't you say anything either. I want to ask some questions, that's all."

"You never did tell me what he looked like," Nicky said.

No way was I describing what I saw, or showing him the picture. "I told you, he was all beaten up. And dirty."

"What else? Did he look like Mr. Grimshaw?"

I thought about it for a moment. "I don't think so. He was a lot younger."

"You should check out Mr. Grimshaw's photos of his family. The ghost might be in them. I mean, as a real person back then."

"Yeah, maybe I will," I said.

I knew King was probably right, that the ghost wasn't about to leave me in peace, but Mr. Grimshaw's family photos might show that the ghost wasn't his relative, but was someone unconnected. I'd have to work out my questions first, so I wouldn't make Mr. Grimshaw suspicious.

I drowned my muesli in more milk and stirred it slowly, remembering how Mum used to love stewed apple and nuts with hers. Was she sitting at a table somewhere up north, eating muesli right now? Was she missing us? Missing me?

My hand jerked, splashing oats and milk onto the table.

She was probably out having a good time in the sports car, enjoying the sunshine up there. She probably couldn't even remember what we looked like anymore.

Who cared about Mum and her stupid muesli? I tipped mine into the trash. I wasn't hungry anymore.

Chapter Eleven

Dad had left early to go back to Mrs. Alsopp's house. He was going to be busy, as her daughter was arriving to look at the house and find out about the case. The fire investigators were still working on the scene, and the local police were meeting with the Melbourne experts after lunch for an update and a plan of action. I wasn't sure who was in charge, maybe the homicide detectives, but it wasn't Dad. He'd be expected to provide local information though, and maybe interview people.

As Nicky and I left the house, it started to rain, and I thought of all the ash and burned things in Mrs. Alsopp's house turning to slurry under the gray sky. The fairytale windows and balconies gone. Her poor daughter, left with nothing but destruction and death. Mrs. Alsopp had seemed kind and full of fun and determined to stay in her home, no matter what. But she hadn't bargained on someone killing her. My thoughts were as dark and rain-filled as the grim sky, and a deep chill soaked through me that had nothing to do with the weather.

I wondered what paintings had been stolen, how the thief had known what was there and what to take. Had she bought anything from the local gallery? Mr. Jones-Sutton said not. Not even the Nolan that I'd seen in my dream.

I stopped abruptly in the middle of the street as we were crossing, and Nicky pulled me out of the way of a car whose driver tooted at me.

"You're worse than a kangaroo," he said.

"What?"

"That's how they get hit – they get hypnotized by headlights."

I shook my head. Mr. Jones-Sutton might not have sold her anything, but he would've known she had some valuable paintings, including the Nolan. He'd visited her. Another realization slammed into me. What about the day *we'd* visited her, and I thought I'd seen one of the doors in the hallway glowing? Had I seen a sign that Mrs. Alsopp's house was going to burn down? How could I possibly have known what the glowing meant?

You couldn't. You're expecting too much of yourself.

As we reached the sidewalk, I stopped again and laid my hand on King's head. *This is driving me nuts. How am I supposed to understand this stuff?*

You're not trained. It's like trying to be a cadaver dog when you don't know what a dead person smells like.

What? I snatched my hand away. *Are you serious?*

Of course. Sorry if my example was a bit ...

Gross.

"Come on, it's wet," Nicky said, even though he had the umbrella, and it was me and King getting rained on.

The museum's bricks were stained by the water dripping from its rusted gutters, and a hole in the roof over the porch let through a steady stream. We dodged the splashes, and Nicky pushed open the door. Inside, extra lights had been turned on, and a gas heater rumbled in the corner; the large room had lost much of its murkiness. It still seemed cold and unfriendly to me, with the gleaming glass cases, stern faces in photos and echoing wooden floor.

"Mr. Grimshaw," Nicky called. "Are you here?"

Somewhere a toilet flushed and water ran, then the old man shuffled out from behind a display board. "Well, well, it's young Nicholas."

"Hello. We've come back."

"I can see that." Mr. Grimshaw's mouth turned up a tiny bit at the ends.

"Sasha wants to ask you some questions, about your great-grandfather."

133

"Does she now?" Mr. Grimshaw's eyes flicked over me and down to King, sitting quietly beside me. "Is that your dog?"

"Yes." I waited for him to tell us to take King outside.

"They're a good, reliable breed, German shepherds. Is he trained?"

"He used to be a police dog," Nicky said. "He's very brave."

King sat up straighter beside me.

"Yes, he is," I said. "He saved me from that horrible Wallace dog." I didn't know why I was telling Mr. Grimshaw, but he nodded with a pleased expression on his face.

"He is a good, brave dog. We could do with more like him around here." His gaze came back to me. "What're your questions, girlie?"

"I ... um ..." I stopped and gathered the threads in my brain. "Nicky and I went inside the old police cell in our backyard."

"The scene of the crime," Mr. Grimshaw said.

"Someone told us that your family has never believed your great-grandfather killed himself. Is that true?"

"You don't mince words, do you?" he said. "Comes of being a copper's kids, I suppose." He turned and walked away, and I thought I'd upset him, but he said over his shoulder, "You two want a cup of tea?"

I didn't really, but if it would make him friendlier and more talkative, I'd drink it. "Yes, please." Nicky skipped ahead of me, chattering to Mr. Grimshaw like they were old friends. Maybe Mr. Grimshaw wasn't rude, like I'd thought, just gruff.

Nicky seemed to like him a lot. I followed slowly, glancing along the line of photos, but they were just a collection of people in old-fashioned clothes to me. King settled down by the heater and closed his eyes.

Five minutes later, we were sitting in a little kitchen area with our big mugs of tea and a package of shortbread, and Mr. Grimshaw started talking. "Albert Jones was my mother's grandfather. He started looking for gold up near Bendigo and lost his claim in a card game, so he decided to venture further afield to make his fortune. In those days, the big gold rush was over, but there were still a few who thought they could find the nugget that'd make them rich."

"Did you know they found a big gold nugget when they were digging up water pipes in the main street last year?" Nicky asked me.

"Here?" I sipped my tea and tried not to grimace.

"No, in Dunolly," Mr. Grimshaw said. "Over on the other side of the ranges. Anyway, my great-grandfather, Albert Jones, came down this way and was digging up in the hills here, around an area where there'd been Chinese miners years before. He found gold, we're sure of it, because he suddenly had money. He must've been taking the gold down to Melbourne to sell it, so no one around here would guess and start following him to find his mine."

"Lots of money?" Nicky asked.

"Enough to open a bank account and put a good amount away." Mr. Grimshaw coughed and promptly got out his tobacco tin and rolled himself a cigarette. The rolling and licking and tamping and lighting took a while, and the smoke as he puffed at it smelled putrid. I put up with it, wanting to hear the rest of the story.

"After a few weeks, as well as buying some new picks and a new hat, Albert decided to risk a bit of a celebration. He went to the pub one night and had a few too many beers, and then some whisky. He staggered out of the pub and passed out in the gutter. Sergeant Williams arrested him and took him back to the cell."

Listening to the rhythm of Mr. Grimshaw's voice, I sensed that this was a story he'd told quite a few times, and I wondered how much it had been exaggerated. How much was even true? But I couldn't ask because that would make the old man angry with me, I was sure.

"Williams knew Albert had struck it rich, and he was determined to get the mine location out of him. He beat Albert up with his truncheon and then strangled him with a strip of cotton sheeting. And then Williams told everyone that Albert had killed himself in a fit of alcoholic remorse."

"How do you know?" Albert's beaten, bloody face flashed through my mind, and I flinched.

"Remorse for what?" Nicky said.

Mr. Grimshaw focused his watery eyes on me like he could see right into my head. "We know because my great-grandmother went and claimed his body, and she said no man in his right mind would beat himself to a pulp first and then hang himself."

Nicky rubbed his jaw like Dad did when he was thinking hard about something. "Sounds very suspect to me, too."

The corners of Mr. Grimshaw's mouth twitched up again. "You're right there, lad. The sergeant said Albert was full of remorse because he had another wife and child back in England, and he'd lied to everyone about it, and he couldn't live with the guilt anymore."

"Was it true?" I said.

"Of course not!" Mr. Grimshaw snapped. "But Williams produced a picture of a woman with a little boy that looked a lot like Albert, and most people were scandalized and believed Williams. My great-grandmother was shunned by half the town and pitied by the other half. She said she didn't know which was worse." He glanced at me. "It's all in her diary, by the way. I've got it safely locked up."

"Did they ever find out the truth?" Nicky asked.

"Years later, my grandmother found out that the photo was one Williams had taken off a dead vagrant. Turned out the vagrant was a wanted murderer, so there were records of his family. Someone had been researching him in the area, and Granny recognized the photo. One in a million chance."

"But too late to help Albert," I said. "And too late to prove anything, I guess."

"Williams was dead by then," Mr. Grimshaw said. "Died of a heart attack. Served him right."

"Mr. Grimshaw still wants to clear Albert's name," Nicky

told me.

"Aye, well, that'd be nice," Mr. Grimshaw said. "Finding out the truth about the photo helped, but Albert's death is still recorded as a suicide. That's what sticks in my gut. They wouldn't let him be buried in the family plot."

"So, what do you think, Sasha?" Nicky smiled at me, obviously hoping that now I'd tell Mr. Grimshaw that I'd seen his ancestor, but how could I possibly describe what he looked like? I'd have to relive it again: Albert's blood, Albert's swollen face, Albert's red, slitted eye staring at me. No way.

I forced a tight smile. "It's a fascinating story."

"It's no story," Mr. Grimshaw said, slapping the table. "It's the truth."

I gripped my mug harder, determined not to argue with him. "Nicky said you had photos we could look at?"

Mr. Grimshaw led me over to a group of photos, including the one of Sergeant Williams I'd seen before, and pointed at a family sitting in front of a dark curtain, all unsmiling. "This is my great-grandmother and her daughter and two sons. This boy here is my grandfather, James." The next photo was of a sturdy-looking woman with a horse and plow. "My great-grandmother on the farm they bought with Albert's money in the bank."

"The sergeant never found out the location of Albert's mine?" I asked.

"No, so the murder was all for nothing."

"And Albert's family never knew where it was?"

He shook his head. "Albert never told a soul."

"Maybe we could find it," Nicky said excitedly.

"Plenty have tried, believe me," said Mr. Grimshaw. "It's probably fallen in by now and lost forever."

The other photos were of the town bank and other buildings. "Have you got any pictures of Albert?" I asked.

"Only one," Mr. Grimshaw said. "He'd been in the army before he came out to Australia." He took the photo out of a drawer in the cabinet under the display and handed it to me. "He's only about eighteen here."

I looked into Albert Jones's smooth, young face under his army cap, and a jolt went through me. It was the man in the cell – younger and unmarked – but I'd know his eyes and the shape of his face anywhere. I'd drawn them, after all. I nearly dropped the photo, and Mr. Grimshaw grabbed it off me. "Careful, girlie, you look like you've seen a ghost."

"She has!" Nicky burst out.

I gasped. "Nicky!" I glared at him – how could he have been so stupid? He'd promised! Then I glanced at Mr. Grimshaw, whose face had gone so pale that the nicotine stain on his top lip was like a yellow stripe. His mouth opened, and I knew he was going to demand that we explain, but I couldn't. I couldn't explain, and I couldn't answer his questions. It was bad enough that *I* knew I was a freak. "I have to go. Thanks for talking to me, Mr. Grimshaw." I turned and ran out of the museum, leaving Nicky behind with the umbrella.

What would Mr. Grimshaw do now? Question Nicky, of course. I wanted to scream. If Nicky went ahead and told him everything, the old man would be hounding me for more. What had Tangine said? He was obsessed with finding out the truth. Now he'd think I knew.

I stopped, and King bumped into the back of my legs, but I barely noticed. How could I tell Mr. Grimshaw what I'd seen? What I'd seen was Albert dying. I couldn't bear to think about it, and I wasn't even related to him. Nicky was such a blabbermouth!

Well, I'd deny it all. I'd say Nicky was making it up, and it was nothing to do with me.

I strode down the street, shoulders back, determined to stick to my decision, no matter what Mr. Grimshaw said. King trotted next to me, and I could feel his anxiety.

You two shouldn't split up. It's not safe. I can't be with both of you.

I stopped again. *Sorry, I forgot.* I turned around and walked back. Near the museum, across from the gallery, were two empty shops with awnings. I could wait for Nicky there, sheltered, but within sight of the museum front door. I huddled in one of the doorways, out of the freezing wind that blew the rain sideways across the street. The lights were on in the gallery, but from this angle, I couldn't see anyone inside. Probably too cold and bitter for tourists today.

At the side of the gallery was a driveway, and a couple of minutes later, a rusty green station wagon slowed and turned in, splashing through puddles, parking under a rickety carport. A man got out, huddling into his coat, and came back down the driveway; he opened a door I hadn't noticed and went inside. He seemed familiar, but I knew I'd never seen him before, and then it struck me. He was a smaller version of Mr. Jones-Sutton. They were either brothers or closely related – the same reddish hair and long, pointy nose. The same surly expression.

King shuffled in behind my legs. *It's freezing out here. Maybe I should go and get Nicky.*

But I didn't want to see Mr. Grimshaw again. I stayed where I was.

The door opened and the red-headed man came out again and opened the trunk of his car. Over the next few minutes, he carried out half a dozen paintings wrapped in clear plastic and stowed them in the station wagon. I was sure two of them were the Boyds, going by the frames and the colors I could see through the plastic. Where was he taking them? Surely they hadn't all been sold? Was he stealing them? No, not in the middle of the day like that. Maybe he was taking them somewhere safer?

Was the Nolan painting among them? No, that was one of those silly assumptions Dad said I made.

The red-headed man closed the trunk and got into the car, reversed out and drove away. Through the car window, his face was screwed up into a ferocious scowl, as if he was angry about the paintings. Or was that me trying too hard to "see" what people were thinking or feeling?

Don't try to work it out, just go with it.

There's something funny going on with the gallery and the stolen paintings, I'm sure. But I don't have any evidence.

Maybe whatever it is that you "see" only happens when it's crucial.

Like someone dying?

Maybe.

I burrowed deeper into my coat and pulled my hat flaps down, but I couldn't hide from what King said. Perhaps I should be grateful that I didn't pick up everyone's thoughts and secrets. My brain was crowded enough already. But if it would help Dad and the homicide detectives solve Mrs. Alsopp's murder … I mentally filed away what I'd seen to think about later.

Across the street, the museum door opened, and Nicky came out, followed by Mr. Grimshaw. Nicky was still talking, and the old man kept nodding, then Nicky put up his umbrella, waved and set off for home. Mr. Grimshaw disappeared back inside. King and I caught up with Nicky near the corner of the street.

"What did you tell him?" I demanded.

Nicky stuck his bottom lip out and wouldn't answer.

"You told him everything, didn't you? After I said not to."

"He didn't believe me anyway," he said. "Said we were making it up."

"So what was all that friendly stuff just now at the door?"

"His dad was a ventriloquist and had an amateur stage show that he toured around the pubs. He was telling me about it." Nicky blinked a few times. "Have you finished yelling at me?"

"Sorry, I didn't mean to." I squeezed his shoulder. "Look, I think I imagined the man in the cell. This town gives me the creeps, and I've been having some bad dreams. Let's forget about it. Hey, I'm dying for some hot chocolate, aren't you?"

"That's not what you said when we came out of the cell." Nicky's face furrowed in concentration. "I think ... I think you did see Albert."

"No, I thought I did, but I did have a big bump on my head." Before the urge to shake him got the better of me, I took my hand off his shoulder.

"I'm not a dumb little kid, you know," he said. "I think you can do stuff like that, see things. And you're trying to pretend you don't."

"That's stupid. You make me sound like one of those crappy TV shows." I tried to laugh, but it stuck in my throat, a prickly ball of fear. *Please, Nicky, give it a rest.* But once he decided he was on to something, he didn't give up easily.

"You could help people with this, you know that?" He tried to hold my hand, like he was comforting me, but I pulled it away. Now I really did want to shake him – instead, I folded my arms tightly.

"I don't want to, Nicky. It's not a fun thing. It's horrible and scary. I just want to be ... normal, you know? Not weird.

Not creeped out."

"It's not creepy, it's exciting," he said, but I could see the cloud of doubt in his eyes.

"Not to me, Nicky. To me, it's really frightening and horrible." Please understand. My hands clenched as I watched his face.

He thought for a moment. "OK, I get it … sort of," he said. "I guess it's not like my magic tricks, is it?"

Relief rippled through me. "Not at all." I made myself smile. "Let's forget about it." I smoothed my hat flaps down with damp hands. "What do you want to do now?"

"Can we go to Tangine's shop, so I can buy my new magic tricks?"

"Where did you get the money?"

"Dad gave it to me. I cleaned up the kitchen and mopped all the floors after he went to work." He sighed theatrically. "Of course, you were still asleep, as usual."

"All right, smarty, I guess we can do that."

The rain eased off as we reached the magic shop, so Nicky put down the umbrella and shook the water off it. "Oh, pooh. The shop's closed." A sign in the door said *Open Tomorrow*, but I was sure I could see someone moving around in the back.

"She's in there. Maybe if you knock, she'll open up for you."

Nicky rapped on the door and waited, but nobody came. "Are you sure you saw her?" he asked.

"I saw someone." Was she avoiding us? Or was it someone else? It could be a burglar, but somehow I doubted it. Tangine obviously wasn't in the mood for visitors. That sure matched with her hot-and-cold attitude to me. "Come on. We'll try again tomorrow."

Nicky sulked all the way home, until I promised to make him some cookies and said he could help. "Anzacs?" he said.

"Have to be. They're the only ones I'm any good at."

"You told Dad you were going to learn how to cook. You should make dinner tonight."

"You're keen on being poisoned, are you?" I said, grinning. But it would give me something to do. Dad probably wouldn't be home until late again. We found flour and oats and honey, and I let Nicky stir it all together. While the Anzac biscuits were in the oven, I grabbed my sketch pad and drew the red-headed man I'd seen at the gallery, then next to him I drew Mr. Jones-Sutton. I'd always been good at recalling faces, and they definitely looked like brothers to me.

To cook a meal that didn't taste like garbage, I needed a recipe of some kind. We still had a couple of Mum's recipe books in a box, but I avoided them – they'd have notes and comments in her handwriting. I picked another book out, one with a picture of a farm on the cover. There was meat in the freezer labeled "stewing steak," so I found a recipe for beef stew that seemed pretty simple and put the meat in the microwave to defrost. When the cookies were ready, we ate them hot, the best way, pigging out on eight each. Then

Nicky went back to watching TV while I wrestled with the beef stew.

At last it was all in the pot, bubbling away, and I sat down to read one of my novels, but my brain kept jumping around from the ghost to Mr. Grimshaw's story to the red-headed man to Mark Wallace and his dog. Why did Mark say his father knew me? Where was the red-headed man taking the paintings? Would Mr. Grimshaw ask me about what I saw in the cell, or would he believe I was lying? Would the police find out who killed Mrs. Alsopp?

The questions bouncing around made me jumpy; I paced the kitchen, pausing to stir the stew, muttering to myself. Dad had said I needed evidence, but I had no way of gathering it. They'd consider I was a kid, and what I saw or heard wouldn't count. I ran my fingers over my stitches, feeling the hair stubble. Had Mrs. Alsopp been hit in the back of the head? I shuddered and tried not to think about that.

Maybe none of the things I'd witnessed were connected, but they were all happening at the same time in a small town. Maybe there *was* a link somewhere. My guess was that Mr. Jones-Sutton was removing his most valuable paintings in case they got stolen, too. But the robberies had been going on since long before we arrived, so why wait until now? Was I suspicious of him because I didn't like him? Why was the red-headed man so angry?

Mrs. Alsopp had lived here all her life. Was there a local person who'd let things get out of hand and was now feeling guilty because she had been murdered? Dad thought someone local was supplying information about the rich houses on the hill. Since Mrs. Alsopp hadn't bought any new paintings, they must've known what she already had and which ones were valuable. Did they know she had an alarm system? Dad said systems in the city were usually connected to a security company that investigated when an alarm went off. Out here, maybe there was no such thing, and you had to deal with your own problem.

Pacing wasn't helping. I sat and drew thumbnail sketches of all the people bumping against each other in my head – all except Albert. One picture of him was enough. Drawing wasn't sensing – it was extracting them from my stupid brain and seeing them more clearly. Dad came in, took off his heavy coat and shoes and searched for his slippers. "It's down to freezing out there," he said. "Might snow tomorrow."

"Snow? You're kidding."

He saw my sketches. "Who are all those people? Wait a minute – that's Arthur Grimshaw. And the Wallace boy. Is that Jones-Sutton from the gallery?"

"No, it's someone else I saw there today. I think it's his brother."

"Yeah, they look alike. What's that delicious smell?"

"Dinner," I said, feeling proud of myself. "I think it'll be edible."

"I could eat a roasted cane toad, I'm so hungry," Dad said.

I grinned. "Yep, that's what I cooked."

Nicky raced into the kitchen. "How's the case going, Dad? Have you arrested anyone yet?"

"No. The forensics and fire investigation guys have gone back to Melbourne, so at least I don't have to stand up there anymore, with my feet like blocks of ice, making sure no one enters the site. But the homicide team is staying." He turned the kettle on. "They've set up in the station, although there's not much room. But it means I can stay abreast of what they need and assist. They agree with me that someone local must be supplying information."

"Any suspects?" I asked, as I put out plates for our stew.

"Not really." He eyed us. "How come you two are asking so many questions all of a sudden?"

"Your cases are the most exciting things that happen around here," I said. "You never know, we might be able to help." I was still thinking about how to gather evidence that Dad would take seriously.

"Hmm. I don't think I'll be sharing too much information with you then," Dad said sternly. "There're things you need to stay out of, and things you really don't need to know."

And he wouldn't say another word about it.

Chapter Twelve

The next morning, it was so cold that King refused to move away from the heater. We turned it up to high and sat next to him, dressed in sweaters and two pairs of socks each, with blankets wrapped around us. It wasn't snowing yet, but it was the coldest I'd ever been. I wouldn't have been surprised to see an icicle on the end of my nose.

Dad ate breakfast with us; then he had to go and help the homicide detectives interview some of the local people. "Of course, they'll think I suspect them of something," he said, and went off muttering about how unpopular he was going to be, and what would happen to the community trust he'd been building up. But I wanted Mrs. Alsopp's murderer to be caught, and offending some of the locals wasn't important compared to that.

He came back at lunchtime, in time to stop me and Nicky having a major fight about DVDs. I refused to watch "Spiderman" for the twentieth time!

"Listen, you two," Dad said. "It's not good for you to be stuck inside all the time anyway, and King needs a run. Come with me."

Outside, he opened the back door of the 4 x 4 to reveal two rusty mountain bikes and two bike helmets. "There," he said. "Transportation, fresh air and exercise, all in one."

Nicky and I stared at each other. It was freezing, and we were both shivering, but at least it was something to do. I was so bored I was ready to try anything, even kill myself on a mountain bike. "Helmets are a must," Dad said. "I don't want to see you without them."

"Yes, Dad."

"So, are you going to have a ride?" He beamed at us expectantly.

"After lunch, Dad," I said. "We're hungry."

"Right-o." He carried the bikes to the front door and propped them up against the porch. The mountain bikes looked huge, but at least they were both girls' ones. Dad said he'd bought them cheap from a man who had an ad up on the deli's bulletin board. After we'd eaten and Dad had gone back to work, we decided to try the bikes out. I called King to come, too.

It's too cold. Is it snowing yet?

No. Dad said you have to stay with us.

"How about we ride around the town a bit," I said to Nicky. "We've only seen the main street so far, and the football field."

It'd been a while since either of us had ridden a bike. Nicky's face set in a determined grimace, he pushed off and sat up on the seat – the bike wobbled so much I was sure he'd fall over, but he steadied it and started pedaling and soon disappeared around the corner. I couldn't let him beat me; I pushed off, wobbled and swerved and had to put my feet down fast before I fell over.

King trotted over to watch closely. *Try again.*

Don't you dare laugh.

I pushed off again, wobbled and straightened, tried to pedal, wobbled and then kept going. The corner was a challenge, but I managed it with only one big swerve and rode all the way to the end of the next street where I caught up with Nicky. King kept up with us, loping along, and I gradually warmed up, although my nose still felt numb.

We rode all around the town, up and down every street, and discovered it was bigger than I thought. Hardly anyone was out in the bitter wind, and I wondered where all the kids our age were. If there was no video arcade in town, maybe they hung out at each other's houses? The place always seemed deserted. It was weird.

By the time we arrived home, I knew every street and

house in Manna Creek, and I also knew where Mark Wallace lived. When I'd seen him as we rode past, sitting in his family room watching TV, my feet jabbed hard at the pedals in case his dog came running out. A dirty white van was parked in their weed-infested driveway, so I guessed Mark's dad was home, too. I wondered if Dad had been to "have a word" yet. I ducked my head down, pedaled faster, and made sure not to go down that street again.

Tangine's shop was still closed, and so was the gallery. Dad's 4 x 4 was back in front of the police station, as were two other cars. When we got inside our house, hot and sweaty from riding, I checked through the kitchen window and could see the two detectives with Dad, talking and pinning papers and photos up on a big board. I was dying to go and look at it, but I knew Dad wouldn't let me.

He brought the two detectives home for dinner, setting up the barbecue in the shed, and they all stood outside in heavy jackets, their breath like small clouds around them as they talked. I caught some snippets that didn't mean much – they were careful not to say anything in front of Nicky or me – but I hoped Dad would tell me later what was happening. The detectives were tough-looking, with that strange expression in their eyes I'd noticed when I'd met policemen in Melbourne who'd been in the force a long time. It was kind of flat and hard, but with deep sadness behind it, and it made me feel really sad, too.

After they went back to their motel, the only one in

Manna Creek, I asked Dad, "Have they got any idea who did it?"

He shook his head. "They're still working on who the local is that's supplying information."

"Had anyone been up to see Mrs. Alsopp recently?"

"According to her daughter, nobody." He eyed me. "Have you heard something?"

"No, Dad, truly. I'd tell you. I just …" He raised his eyebrows at me. "It's that Jones-Sutton man. He's a fake. And he did tell you he'd been in her house, so he'd know what paintings she had."

Dad patted my arm, like I was a little kid who had to be humored. "They've checked him out pretty thoroughly. He's owned galleries for years, and has another one in Melbourne. Does quite well, too."

I couldn't tell Dad that Mr. Jones-Sutton felt *wrong* to me, so I shrugged. "Maybe he is OK. Did you find out who the other man is?"

"You were right – he's Jones-Sutton's brother. But he checks out, too. He's a painter, sells quite a bit of work."

"I hope he paints better than his brother." I gave Dad a hug. "I'm going to bed."

But as I lay snuggled under my quilt, with King on the mat beside me, the *wrong* feeling persisted, like a cockroach wriggling away under a dish towel on the sink. I didn't know what it was about the gallery and the two men, but I'd keep my ears and eyes and senses open all the same.

Don't get too close. If they are involved, they're dangerous.

Yes, boss.

Smarty. King closed his eyes.

The sound of the phone woke me, and I blinked, focusing on my clock. 6:10 a.m. I sat up and staggered out of bed, still half-asleep, to find Dad dressed and on his way out.

"Whassup?"

"Go back to bed, Sasha. There's been another break-in. I'll call you soon and let you know what I'm doing, all right?"

"Mmm. Whose house?"

"Connor Jacobson's. He's going to be a very unhappy man. See you later."

I crawled back into bed and tried to remember who Connor Jacobson was. Oh, yes, the big house with the tennis courts. Where there'd been an attempt a few nights ago. Wasn't there a caretaker in that house? What had happened to him? What had been stolen? Paintings again?

For goodness sake, calm down. Your brain is like a washing machine, thumping around.

Sorry.

I tried to stop thinking and block my mind off from King, but I could tell it wasn't working. He kept twitching and lifting his head and glaring at me. In the end I got out of bed, had a shower and dressed in several layers of clothes while standing in front of the heater.

Aren't you cold with no fur?

I quickly folded my arms. *Don't be rude.*

Just curious.

I trudged into the kitchen and made half a dozen slices of toast, yawning widely, and gave him one with honey on it. *Maybe you shouldn't eat toast.*

Nothing wrong with it.

It was gone in two gulps anyway. I checked out the window, but the homicide detectives were obviously not early risers. A spare key to the station was in Dad's room, and I was so tempted to creep in and have a look at their case board, to see who their suspects were, but I knew I'd get in huge trouble if they caught me. A few minutes later, they arrived and let themselves in, so it was just as well I'd resisted.

The day stretched in front of me again, and I ticked off the possibilities: bike riding, cooking, watching TV. I hadn't been on the Net for ages, mainly because I didn't want to find my only emails were from stupid spammers. A twinge of loneliness pinched at me – I wished I had someone my own age to talk to and hang out with. Mark Wallace? A giggle spluttered in my throat and died. Maybe he was the only person in Manna Creek who … no, don't go there. Even anonymous Internet friends would be better than him.

Would I meet any girls at my new school? I was supposed to start there with what Dad called "a clean slate." There was the girl I saw in the car, and there must be more in the town – perhaps they only emerged in the summer. I switched on the computer and connected to the Net, groaning at how slow it was. My one real email was from my old school principal, wishing me well in my new home. It cheered me up for about two seconds, until I remembered all the friends I used to have there, and then I felt depressed again.

It suddenly occurred to me that I could look up Mr. Jones-Sutton and the Boyd paintings. I put in his name and the words *art gallery paintings*, and dozens of entries came up. They were mainly sales records, although his gallery in Melbourne had a basic website that he obviously hadn't spent much money on.

Most of the paintings shown on his site had *Sold* next to them, but I couldn't tell when or for how much. I couldn't see either of the Arthur Boyd paintings from his gallery in Manna Creek, but there were several other Boyds that he'd sold in Melbourne. Maybe that's where they were being taken – back to the city where there were more buyers. And not as many thieves.

I wondered how many paintings he'd sold in Manna Creek since the gallery had opened. Obviously a few, since he'd complained to Dad that they were the ones being stolen.

"What are you doing?" Nicky said, making me jump. "Are you going to paint things to sell? I wouldn't be letting that man sell them."

"He wouldn't anyway," I said. "I was checking him out. Dad said he had a gallery in Melbourne, too."

Nicky was more interested in eating breakfast, so he left

me to it. Had Mr. Jacobson bought any of Mr. Jones-Sutton's paintings? More to the point, had any of them been stolen last night?

I had to wait until Dad arrived home for the answer to that. The homicide detectives were out somewhere, so Dad came straight in to eat lunch with us, putting his file down on the table.

"What happened?" I asked.

"The caretaker, Parker, was away. Sick mother, he said." Dad munched on his cheese and pickle sandwich. "He discovered the break-in when he came back early this morning to have a shower and change his clothes. Said he'd been at the hospital in Marberry all night, so it looks like he's got a good alibi."

"Do you think he was part of it?"

"Maybe, but I doubt it. The key is who knew he wasn't there."

"I bet Mrs. Sullivan at the post office knew," Nicky said.

"Yes, no doubt," Dad said. "She's not a suspect, though."

"How many paintings were taken?" I asked.

"Ten. Altogether worth about a million dollars."

I pointed at the file. "Are they listed in there?"

"Yes, photos, too, from Jacobson's records. I suppose you can look if you want."

I pulled the photos out, going through them slowly. "That's a Joy Hester, and that one's a Fred Williams. And these Aboriginal paintings would be worth a lot, too." I got to the last two paintings and stopped. "Hang on, how could these be stolen? They were in Mr. Jones-Sutton's gallery two days ago."

"What?" Dad took the photos I was holding and turned them over. "No, this says they were bought about a month ago."

"No way." I pointed to the one with the chip off the edge of the frame. "I remember that chip. I wondered why they hadn't reframed it. And I'm one hundred percent sure that they were both still for sale when we looked at them."

Dad fetched a magnifying glass and examined the chip. I held my breath, waiting for him to realize that my suspicions were right.

Chapter Thirteen

Dad put the magnifying glass and photo down and shook his head. "They could have been sold to Jacobson but not picked up yet."

I wanted to strangle him – why was he being such a … a policeman? "No, when a painting is sold in a gallery, they put a red dot on it, or something similar, so other customers know." I tapped the photo, my finger on the chip. "Those paintings had no dots on them. But …"

Right then, I remembered the red-headed man carrying the paintings out to his car. Maybe he was delivering them to Jacobson's house? No, I was certain he wasn't, and if I told Dad about it now, he'd decide that was the answer. I wanted him to stay suspicious.

"But what?" Dad asked.

I bit my lip. I wasn't really lying, just holding something back. "I think the gallery man or Jacobson are up to something." It sounded lame.

"Well, I can't figure out what," Dad said. "It could just be an error on Jones-Sutton's part. Jacobson is a rich man. What would he get out of losing valuable paintings?"

"Insurance money?" I said.

"Why would he need it? He's a multimillionaire, with about four houses and twenty cars." Dad was still using his slow, nit-picking tone. "I can't see it somehow. There's no motive."

"But you always said that everything should be checked out because you never know where the vital information will be hiding," Nicky piped up.

"Yeah, Dad," I said. Nicky was a star, backing me up. I kept glaring at Dad – I wasn't going to let him off the hook.

Dad put up his hands in surrender. "All right, all right, I'll make some enquiries. Will that make you happy?"

I nodded. "Are you going to ask Mr. Jones-Sutton some questions, too?"

"I suppose I'd better, Sergeant Sasha, ma'am." Dad smiled grimly. "And won't that be a pleasant experience. I'll get him to come to the station and make it official."

After lunch, Dad went back to the station, and I saw him on the phone a few minutes later. I pretended I was cleaning up the kitchen, wiping counters and shelves over and over – as soon as I saw Mr. Jones-Sutton's car pull up near the station, I scooted out across the yard, avoiding the cell, and opened the back door of the station.

"Do you want a cup of tea, Dad?" I called.

"No thanks," Dad said. "Mr. Jones-Sutton is here."

"OK." I sneaked in and closed the door loudly, then hid in the little bathroom area where the mop and broom were kept. If Dad caught me, I'd be in major trouble, but I *had* to find out what was said. Sure enough, Mr. Jones-Sutton's voice was so loud that I had no trouble eavesdropping.

"What's this about?" he said. "I've just heard that Connor Jacobson's house has been robbed. And some of my paintings have been stolen. This is outrageous! And it's even more outrageous that you so-called detectives can't catch these criminals."

"We're gathering more information all the time," Dad said. "I thought you might be able to help."

"Of course I will, if I can. But Jacobson's a very good client, and my reputation is suffering."

"I can't quite see how," Dad said. "You're surely not responsible for the thefts, are you?"

"Of course not! How dare you insinuate any such thing!"

I could imagine Mr. Jones-Sutton at this point, beet-red and spitting, his red moustache twitching like a dying caterpillar. Dad didn't let him get away with the tantrum.

"It's a fair question, sir. The detectives have to look at

every angle. After all, every robbery so far has included paintings from your gallery."

"Of course, it's a huge problem for me. I may have to close down this gallery altogether and go back to Melbourne."

He was saying "of course" a lot, as if everything was obvious, but I thought Dad was getting suspicious at last.

"I believe that you recently sold two paintings by Arthur Boyd to Mr. Jacobson, is that right?"

"It is. Arthur Boyd is one of Australia's finest artists, and his landscapes are –"

"Yes, I know." Dad cut him off. "On what date did you sell the paintings?"

"I can't be expected to remember exactly."

"Approximately, then."

"About a month ago, I believe."

"Then how do you explain the fact that those paintings were seen in your gallery a couple of days ago."

"By whom?"

"A visitor."

I started – Dad meant me – and behind me a broom teetered. I snatched at it, my fingers hitting the handle and getting a grip just before it hit the floor. I held my breath and lowered it silently to the tiles.

"They were wrong. The two paintings in my gallery were different ones. You must know that Arthur Boyd painted many different versions of the same scene. I handle quite a few Boyds, and they are all cataloged correctly, I assure you."

I waited for Dad to move in and pick Mr. Jones-Sutton's story to bits. I'd identified the frame as much as the painting. He was definitely lying. But Dad let him off the hook! I wanted to run in and grab the man and shake the truth out of him.

"Perhaps Mr. Jacobson will come back and buy the other ones then, when his insurance payout has been settled."

"Yes, well, I doubt it very much, thanks to the thieves around here! Good day to you."

The station door slammed, and I heard his car roar off, scattering gravel.

"You can come out now," Dad said.

Oops. I sidled into the main room and found Dad turning the homicide board away so I couldn't see it. He poked at one of the photos, re-pinned it and then frowned at me. "You shouldn't be listening in to police business, Sasha."

"Yeah, but he was lying! And you never said anything about the chip in the frame." It was hard to stay calm when Dad didn't seem to see what was right in front of him.

"I don't have any evidence yet. And I didn't want to put him on the alert either." He humphed to himself. "He's carrying on far too much as the injured party, for very little reason. And if you're right about the frame, then he certainly did lie about when he sold that painting. The question is, why?"

"I'm totally sure about the frame, Dad." I thought for a moment. "Why don't you Google Connor Jacobson and see what he's been up to lately?"

"Can't hurt, I suppose." Dad opened his Internet browser and typed in *Connor Jacobson* and the year. Several dozen hits came up, but I scanned them quickly, a page at a time, and found something on the third page. "Look at this. The financial pages from last Friday."

Dad clicked on the link, and we read the article. "His company was stopped from trading shares," Dad said. "That could mean anything."

"Try some of the other links," I said. "Recent news takes a while to get into Google sometimes, unless it's someone famous." On the next page we found a small piece from three days before. "The banks have appointed a liquidator. Doesn't that mean he's going down the tubes?"

Dad nodded. "That could be our motive for this robbery. But it doesn't explain the others, or Mrs. Alsopp's death. Something doesn't fit here."

"It will, if you get more information, and if you find out who the thieves are." I waved my arms around. "They're out there, I know it."

"Yes, but that's not my job here, remember?" Dad bookmarked the links and printed out the articles. "I'll talk to the different detectives handling the robberies and the homicide. They have far more resources than me, and besides, it's their job to find out who killed Mrs. Alsopp."

"Don't you *want* to solve the robberies and her murder?"

Dad grinned. "What – and be the local hero? No, thanks, Sasha. I'm here to be a country policeman, not someone from

'Law and Order.'"

"But –"

"And you stay out of it, too. It's all very well doing a bit of detective work, but you forget that poor old Mrs. Alsopp is dead. These guys aren't playing games. They're serious about getting rid of anyone in their way. The homicide guys think she may have heard the burglar and tried to stop him." He glanced out the back window. "Nicky's waving at us. Why don't you take him and King for a ride on your bikes?"

"It's freezing outside." And I wanted to stay close to Dad – I knew I could help him with information if I had the chance.

"Yes, they're still forecasting snow. Away you go – get some fresh air before the weather really sets in." He shepherded me towards the back door and closed it after me. I heard the lock click home.

I wasn't in the mood for numb fingers, toes and nose, but Nicky was keen and so was King.

A run! Yes, let's go. Bring a tennis ball.

Riding our bikes was easier than walking, but the wind chill was excruciating. I wrapped my scarf around my face and pulled my Lapland hat as far down as I could. King bounded along in front of our bikes as we headed for the football field where we could throw the ball for him. After ten minutes of standing there while he raced back and forth, I said, my teeth chattering, "Come on. I'm turning into an icicle. Let's ride again."

It wasn't raining, but the sky was dark gray, with clouds low over the hills. A freezing gale blew down the main street, cutting through my clothes like an icy knife. As we turned the corner near the deli, a dirty white van zoomed past us, smoke gusting from its exhaust, and I glimpsed the greasy-haired man driving, gloved hands high on the wheel. He turned his head and glared at me, his dark eyes like bits of coal above his big nose. Yes, he was Mark Wallace's dad all right. I jammed on my brakes and gripped the handlebars, trying to tell myself that the Wallaces were scum, and they didn't scare me at all.

Where was he going in such a hurry? He took the road that went up towards the hills – halfway up, it forked. One way took you to where the big houses were, the other wound into thick bush and eventually to the state forest area. Maybe he was one of the art thieves, but somehow I imagined them to be sophisticated and clever, and Mark Wallace's dad was neither. He looked like someone who worked on a farm, or in an outdoors job; I couldn't see him stealing paintings and selling them on the black market.

But I could see him being a local contact, driving around the area, listening in the pub, passing on information about who was away and who lived in the big houses. Had Dad or the detectives investigated him?

In the main street, there were lights on in Tangine's shop, but the *Open Tomorrow* sign was still up, and when we knocked, nobody answered. "Where is she?" Nicky said. "She promised to save those magic tricks for me."

"Who knows?" I said. "I'm quite sure she won't have sold them to anyone else."

Or if we're lucky, she will have. Nicky had been practicing his tricks with King as his audience.

I laughed, and Nicky said, "What?"

"Nothing. Let's go." At home, I searched through the freezer for something easy to cook for dinner and found lamb chops. Surely I could manage to grill those?

I'd just defrosted them in the microwave when Dad came rushing through from the station. "Listen, kids, I've got to go out on an urgent call. I don't know how long I'll be. Those chops look good, Sasha. Save some dinner for me, all right?"

"Mr. Jones-Sutton on the run?" I asked.

"No, I've had a tip-off about the marijuana grower up in the bush. He's harvesting and moving out because of the snow forecast. If I don't nab him right now, he'll go underground until spring." Dad pulled on his all-weather police jacket and hunted for his gloves, which were on top of the fridge. "I'll call you if there's a problem."

"Did you ring for –" He was gone before I could finish, "– backup?" I bit my lip, thinking hard. I'd seen Mr. Wallace drive up into the bush. I should've told Dad right away, and now I didn't know what to do. Would he be mad and tell me I had no evidence? Mr. Wallace could be going anywhere.

King followed me as I paced. *Remember the other day? I smelled marijuana on him.*

King's words brought me to a sudden stop. *I can't stand this. I think I should call Dad.* I dialed his mobile phone, but it said he was currently unavailable, which meant he was in a black spot, out of range. I'd wait a few minutes and try again.

"We'd better lock the doors," Nicky said.

"You do the back door." I double-locked the front, opening it first to peer out into the thick, gray dusk, waiting and listening for a few long seconds. The way Dad ran out of the house bothered me. He hadn't taken his woolly hat, for a start, and he rarely rushed around like that. What if he hadn't called for backup? What if they were late getting there?

No, that was silly. Dad was careful and followed all the rules. If he hadn't called already, he'd do it on the way there with the radio in the 4 x 4. I tried his phone several more times and got the same answer. I knew there were lots of black spots in the area, but that made me feel more agitated, not less.

I busied myself cooking dinner, we ate, and King persuaded me to make him some toast and honey since he wasn't allowed to have the chop bones. Still Dad hadn't come home or called. Nicky and I both took turns peering through the window – night had long since fallen, and it was pitch black outside. King padded back and forth, following us around the house. I checked my watch every ten seconds, it seemed like, and the canned laughter from the TV made me want to kick in the screen.

A feeling was growing inside me, black tendrils that snaked through my guts and up to my brain. Something was dangerously wrong. Was it the gift telling me? Or common sense? I knew Dad was careful, but someone out there had it in for us, especially for him. The sheep's head, the rock, the threat in Mr. Sutton-Jones's voice, Mrs. Alsopp bashed and burned.

I have to do something!

Think it through. If you don't want to use the gift, be logical.

I checked the clock – 9 p.m. – and closed my eyes. Be logical. The police station was closed, and the homicide detectives had either gone back to their motel or back to Melbourne, so I couldn't ask them. What could they tell me anyway? Dad's phone was still out of range. I made a decision and dialed the number for the Marberry station with trembling fingers.

"Marberry Police, Constable Wang speaking."

"Hi, um, this is Sasha Miller. My dad's the policeman here at Manna Creek."

"Hi, Sasha. How are you? Is it snowing there yet?"

"I don't think so. I wanted to know if Dad had called you for backup, maybe around 4 p.m.?"

"Not that I know of. I'll go and check."

My stomach plummeted, and I had to sit down. He came back a couple of minutes later. "No, we haven't heard from him all day. What's happened? Where's he gone?"

The air had vanished from my lungs, and it took a few seconds to suck in some more so I could talk. "He … he said he'd had a tip about someone who's growing marijuana around here, and he raced off to catch them."

"Oh. Right. Hang on."

This time I heard a lot of talking in the background and then someone new came on. "This is Sergeant Pollock, Sasha. Do you have any idea where your dad might've gone?"

Tears welled up in my eyes, and I brushed them away roughly before I answered. "No. Only that it was in the bush, and they were packing up the marijuana because of the snow forecast."

"He didn't call us for backup. Did he say he would?"

"That's why–" I gulped and coughed, tried again. "That's why I think there's something wrong. Dad wouldn't go it alone like that."

More muffled talking, then, "We're sending two units over now. Are you at home?"

"Yes."

"Wait there until we arrive, all right?"

"OK."

I hung up and stared at the side of the fridge that was already covered in magnets and photos. There was Dad, fishing on the bay, his old floppy sun hat looking like a bowl stuck on his head.

Dad, where are you?

Chapter Fourteen

As I sat next to the phone, staring at Dad's photo, Nicky pulled on my arm. "What's going on? Where's Dad?"

"I don't know. The Marberry police are coming over to look for him."

"What? Is Dad in trouble? Can we help?"

"We don't know where he is." And he didn't take his hat.

Nicky's face lit up. "Let's send King out to find him."

King looked at me, his ears forward. *Not possible. No scent.*

"Dad went in his 4 x 4. It won't have left a scent like a person does." I went to the front door and unlocked and opened it, staring out, wishing Dad would pull up in the street right that minute, laughing and saying how cold his head was, and why hadn't I reminded him about his hat. But instead a thin, soupy rain drifted down.

"It's not going to snow after all," Nicky said.

"Thank goodness. But that stuff feels as cold as snow." The temperature had dropped again, and the skin on my face felt brittle and tight.

Where was Dad? Surely he wasn't out in the bush somewhere in this?

I kept trying his mobile and pacing through the house. Nicky took up a vigil at the family room window, his face reflecting like a pale moon. Twenty minutes later the Marberry police arrived, and the man who came to the door said he was Sergeant Pollock. He carried a map of the area that he brought inside and spread out on the table, and his grim face made my tiny flame of hope flicker and die.

"You haven't heard from him yet?" he asked.

"No. Have you?"

"No." He stared down at the map. "We've tried the radio in his vehicle, but there's no response." He pointed at a road that led into the state forest north of Manna Creek. "We'd heard the plantation was in here. Is that where your dad went?"

"He didn't say. I'm sorry." Why hadn't I asked him where he was going? Why had I let him rush out like that? My chin trembled, and I bit my bottom lip hard to stop myself from crying.

"It's the best option and it ties in with other information. Even though that never ..." He snapped his mouth shut and folded up the map. "You kids need to stay here, in case he calls. This is my mobile number. Let me know as soon as you hear from him."

He gave me his card, and I didn't bother to remind him that there were lots of places where mobile phones didn't work around here. He'd know that already. Both cars left, lights flashing, turning our family room strangely red and blue for a few seconds. I felt the black tendrils of dread snake around my heart and squeeze hard.

"I'm scared, Sasha," Nicky said. "What if something has happened to Dad? Something bad?"

"Dad'll be fine." I forced a smile onto my face that hurt my mouth. "He's sensible and tough, remember? The best combination."

"You reckon?"

"Yep." But I wasn't so sure. Especially that now it was raining. Dad never left us for more than a couple of hours without calling in. It wasn't just the mobile signal coverage. But I didn't want Nicky to know how scared and worried I was. "How about some ice cream and chocolate sauce?"

I tried to keep Nicky distracted, and even let him show me two tricks I'd seen him mess up a hundred times, and he messed them up again. Usually I groaned at him, but this time I said, "Never mind, I'm sure it'll work next time, with a bit more practice." He curled up on the couch with a blanket to watch TV, looking about four years old, the fear still a shadow in his eyes. The loneliness I'd felt before fell on me again, this time like a glacial avalanche. There was no one I could call, nobody at all. Not even Mum. I squeezed my eyes shut, trying to think positive, trying to imagine Dad walking in through the door, laughing and complaining about the weather. It didn't work.

I needed something to do and went to the kitchen to make a big mug of hot chocolate for each of us.

King followed me in. *This is a dangerous situation.*

I know, but what can I do?

You need to look for him.

The other police are doing that already. They'll be mad if I butt in.

Not like that. I mean look. *You might be able to see where he is.*

Look? Oh. That. My brain rejected the idea immediately, but the black creepers loosened a little.

Yes. That.

But …

Did I really want to encourage the gift like this? It might let something bigger loose, something I couldn't control. Nightmares, visions, horrible deaths – taking over, leaving me terrified and helpless. And treated as evil or crazy. Why would I bring that down on myself?

But King was right about looking for Dad. Did I have any option? I glanced out at the old cell, just a shadow in the back of the yard, and shivered. What if Albert showed up instead? But I'd never seen or sensed Albert anywhere else but the cell.

All the same, he haunted me, I dreamed about him, like I still saw the man being hit by the bus. I couldn't get rid of them, and if I kept on like this, I'd have more dead people jostling for space inside my head.

But I don't see dead people, I see people about to die. What if I see Dad getting murdered?

The thought was like an electric shock, a huge zap that left me open-mouthed and gasping. Dad dying? I crashed down onto a chair, my hands on the table gripping each other so tightly my knuckles cracked.

No, that was stupid. I'm making things worse. Calm down. Think! The truth was, if I didn't try this, and Dad died, I'd never forgive myself. I'd always wonder if I could've saved him.

Take it easy. Settle down. King's voice was soothing, helping me to calm my brain.

OK, I need to do this. I need to try. Oh, please, let it work the right way for a change!

I closed my eyes, flattened my palms on the table and tried to focus on Dad, but instead I kept seeing the greasy-haired man, Mark Wallace's dad. Why was I thinking of him? Because he was dying? Or hurting Dad?

No, because we saw him on the waterfall trail.

And you said he smelled of marijuana. So if Dad went to find the marijuana plants in his 4 x 4, he'd be heading up the hill, the back road past the creek. Not where the police went.

I looked around for a map, but the only one we had was

on the wall in the station. I found the spare key in Dad's room and headed across the backyard, King following me. As I neared the cell, my head started to feel heavy and achy, but I walked faster and concentrated on unlocking the back door.

The map was on the wall by the counter, and I found the main street, then traced the creek down to the waterfall and further along the valley. The trail started by following the creek, but then it forked several times as it wound up into the hills. I doubted Dad would've walked in on the waterfall trail – his phone wouldn't have stopped working so fast, and his 4 x 4 would be parked in town. I followed the hills road out to the first intersection and ran my finger back across the large area of bush to the waterfall. There were two possible trails in that part, squiggly brown lines through the green, and both of them also were near a dead-end road. "Dad could've gone up here. It's closer." As I jabbed my finger at Gold Diggers Lane, a sense of certainty grew inside me. I knew that's where he'd gone, I *knew* it. "I'd better call Sergeant Pollock and tell him."

But when I went back to our house and called his number, all I got was a message saying the person I was calling was out of range. I wanted to scream with frustration and banged the phone down. "What now?"

Sit down and focus on your father. Breathe. Stop panicking.

That's easy for you to say!

Dogs rarely panic.

I glared at him.

All right, I did once. It won't happen again. Sit.

176

I did as he said, placed both hands on the table and closed my eyes again. *Breathe. Calm down. Dad. Where are you? Are you in trouble? Dad?*

Nothing came.

I can't see anything! Stupid gift is gone!

King came close and laid his muzzle on my thigh. *I'll help. Think of your dad. Imagine his face. Think about what he looked like when he left earlier.*

I took a few breaths and tried to settle. *Dad.* He'd been wearing his warm jacket; he'd taken his phone, but he hadn't called us.

Dad. Where are you?

For a few long moments, there was nothing, just dark gray patterns swirling in front of me like always. A worm of panic slithered upwards from my stomach, and I almost stopped. *Focus. Keep trying.* A flash of something came and went. Was it him? I tried to breathe slowly, opening my mind, waiting, waiting.

Then I saw Dad, lying on the ground. He was totally still, drizzle falling on him, soaking his jacket. Was he dead? Every shred of me arrowed in on him, trying to sense what was happening. He was breathing, but he was really cold. Blood on his head. Someone had hit him. He was unconscious.

King nudged me. *Where?*

I angled out, looked around. Gum trees. They all looked the same. *I don't know where he is! We have to go out there. Now!*

How will you find him?

Maybe I'll see more as I get closer. We have to try.

I jumped up and ran to get my coat, hat and scarf. In the kitchen cupboard was a heavy flashlight that I tucked under my arm. Nicky looked up from the TV, his face puzzled. "Where are you going?"

"I think I know where Dad is, and it's not where the police went. And I can't phone them." I sat next to him on the couch, gave him a quick hug, desperate to go, but wanting to try and reassure him first. It was like a tug-of-war inside me. "I have to go and try, Nicky."

"I want to come." His chin jutted out.

"You can't." I had to think fast. "We need someone to be here, in case Dad calls, or the other police call in. And you have to keep trying Sergeant Pollock, too. That's an important job."

"No, it's not. If it was, you'd do it."

Oh, no, he was being stubborn. I didn't have time for this. Impatience fizzed through me. "It is important, Nicky. And you also have to make another call for Dad, too."

"What?"

"You have to call Marberry station and tell them this." I explained about the new location I'd come up with, and why. "Can you remember all that? And you might have to call Melbourne, too, if they want you to."

"Oh. All right. Is King going with you?"

"He'll stay here with you."

King barked and glared at me indignantly. *No, I won't. I*

have to come with you. I can track; you can't.

I stopped, thought about it: the eerie bush; the wet, icy rain; the dark trails. I could so easily get lost and freeze to death, like Dad. "Now that I think about it, I'm going to need King to help me. Will you be all right on your own?"

"Sure. I'm cool." But he didn't look so cool. If Nicky kept the doors locked, he should be fine. I told myself that three times until I believed it without feeling massively guilty.

"Thanks, Nicky. You're being really brave and a big help."

"Yeah." He still sounded unsure, but there was no time to waste trying to make him feel better. I kept seeing Dad lying in the snow and the blood on his head. *I'm coming, Dad.*

It would take me forever to walk to where I thought he might be, even if I went through the bush via the waterfall trail. And I didn't want to go that way – it'd be slippery and dangerous. I didn't need another fall and crack on the head. I'd have to take the bike. I wheeled it out into the street and hopped on; the icy drizzle was like a moving, slippery fog that clung to my face, and I hoped it wouldn't make the bike impossible to ride. Thank goodness Dad had bought bikes with headlights on them, although the beam struggled to light up the road ahead.

The town was deserted, but the streetlights gave me some help. A throaty exhaust muttered somewhere near me, and I caught a glimpse of a familiar dirty white van turning in behind Tangine's shop. What was Mr. Wallace doing there? A flurry of heavy rain poured down on me, and I ducked my

179

head and pedaled harder, riding out beyond the last lights.

King and I took the hill road out of town, the same way the Marberry police had gone, but after a few hundred yards we turned left down Gold Diggers Lane. It went from asphalt to gravel, and I stayed in the middle, pedaling hard to get up the rise. The road had turned to muddy slush, and the bike slid and jagged – the drizzle had increased to a light rain blown by the wind, and ice-cold trickles ran down the inside of my collar. I needed a moleskin jacket or thick raincoat, but all I had was my padded jacket. I wouldn't be able to stay out long in that, or I'd end up worse off than Dad.

How far do we go along here?

To the end. It's not a long road, according to the map.

Feet are cold.

Mine, too.

Everything was cold. My fingers were almost numb inside my gloves. At least the hard pedaling was keeping me sort of warm. King splashed along next to me, his head down, mud splattering up his legs. Over the next rise, the road came to an end, and there was Dad's 4 x 4.

"Yes!" I shouted. "I was right."

Where is he?

We stopped next to the 4 x 4 and opened the driver's door; it was empty, and the keys weren't in the ignition. If the worst came to the worst, I could shelter inside it, but without being able to start the engine, there'd be no heating.

Radio?

Of course. Dad's radio inside should be able to pick up Marberry station or the other cars. But when I leaned across to turn it on, the lights stayed off. It was dead.

Stop and think about this.

There's no time! Already I was peering into the bush, my heart racing. Where was Dad? Which way should I go?

Sasha, you're panicking! Settle down. If your father went into the bush to find the marijuana plantation, why didn't he use his radio?

It's not working.

Why not? It's standard equipment. He wouldn't have wandered away without calling someone, once he knew the radio was dead. He's a rules man, remember?

"Um …" King was right. It was only someone growing marijuana. If Dad had gone off searching on his own, he must've thought it was really urgent. What could it be? Had he found Mrs. Alsopp's murderer?

Who knew he was coming here?

I had seen Dad lying on the ground, and I knew that he'd been hit on the head. I'd assumed it had happened when he'd found the growers. But what if it wasn't them? What if it had been a setup to get Dad out of the way? What if it was Jones-Sutton, and it was my fault that Dad had been suspicious of him?

I still don't understand why Dad would go in on his own. What happened?

In this weather, he probably wouldn't have noticed anyone

181

following him. Can you see where he is? Is anyone else there?

I closed my eyes. There he was, the same as before. Was I remembering, or was I seeing something new? No, he was soaked through now. He'd been there a while.

He's on a slope, with big rocks further up. He's alone. Whoever attacked him has gone. I peered past the 4 x 4 and saw the start of the trail. *We have to find him. Will there be a scent?*

King whined. *The rain will have probably washed it away. But I'll do my best. The rest is up to you.*

Let's go then.

I shut the door, turned on my flashlight, and we set off along the narrow trail. Despite the rain, there were a couple of boot prints in the mud, and crushed bracken and grass – signs of recent use. The boot patterns were different, but I couldn't tell if the second person was ahead of Dad or behind him. King surged ahead of me, nose to the ground. I tried to jog, but the trail was slippery. Careful and fast – it was impossible! Under the tree canopy, the rain eased off a bit, but there were still huge splatters of water falling from leaves above. The gray-black trees closed in around us, their trunks streaked with wetness. The trail was covered in wet leaves and twigs, and I slipped sideways, gasping as pain shot through my ankle. I rubbed it hard, kept going, and it seemed OK. After a couple of minutes I paused to listen, and the thick silence felt ominous, like the eye of a horrific storm was about to turn on us. My panting was swallowed up as if I didn't exist. I called King. *Wait. Listen.*

"Dad!" I yelled, my voice breaking. "Dad!" My calls were sucked in between the monster trees and devoured whole.

Keep moving. Too cold to stand still.

We came to a fork, and I had no idea which trail to follow.

Give me a minute. King went off down one trail, came back and tried the other. It was steeper, climbing upwards. *No scent on either. It's up to you.*

I closed my eyes, putting my gloved hands over my face to stop the cold and rain distracting me. *Dad, which way did you go?* I saw him briefly again, and when I took my hands away and looked at the trails, the left one seemed sharper and clearer. *Go left.*

Are you sure?

Nearly.

Was nearly good enough? What if we wasted an hour and Dad died? My head was about to explode with all the *what-ifs*, but I forced my feet to go left. The trail was muddier on the side, but there were no boot prints, only some gouges and scrapes. I couldn't tell if they were recent, or if we were going the right way. About fifty yards further on, we came to the creek. It was running high, dirty and full of leaves and debris. The only way across was a fallen tree trunk.

Can you cross on that?

Yes. Can you?

I looked around. There was no other option, and the water was too high to wade. *I think so.* But were we going the right way? Yes. I had a strong flash of Dad again, lying so still that I let out a whimper. I knew I had to keep going, pretend the tree was a wide bridge. The wind was blowing again in sharp gusts, and I cursed it under my breath.

Halfway across, the tree branches afforded handholds, but first I had to get that far. King stepped across, slipping a couple of times, but his paws were steady, and he reached the other side. My feet were a different story, but at least I had tennis shoes on. My leather boots would've been a death trap. My arms flailed around as I tried to balance on the trunk. Every step took me ages, and King watched anxiously. At last I reached the first branch and had something to hang on to, but the rest of it was no better; a bit further along, I slipped, my leg sliding down, and I banged my knee hard against a branch. Pain spiked up the side of my kneecap, and I clung to a branch for a few seconds, muttering rude words under my breath. Finally, I made it across and limped up the creek bank behind King.

This way. He leaped forward, bounding up the trail, skidding in the wet leaves. Something had changed, like a light had switched on inside him. I followed him as fast as I could, hobbling and rubbing my knee, but he left me behind in a few minutes, racing away around a corner.

Wait!

I've found him. Hurry.

Chapter Fifteen

I broke into a staggering run along the trail, my heart thumping hard, barely feeling the pain. Sure enough, near another fallen gum tree, there was Dad, lying just as I'd seen him. I dropped to the ground beside him, my hands shaking uncontrollably as I reached out to touch him. My fingers brushed his temple. His face was white, and he was completely still. I shuddered, sitting on the wet trail, numbness seeping through me. He couldn't be dead, he couldn't be!

He's been hit in the head. King nudged Dad's arm. *He needs to wake up.*

But isn't he …

King growled and glared at me. *Don't be silly.* He nudged again, his muzzle pushing at Dad's face. *Come on, do something.*

I leaned forward, pulling a glove off, and ran my fingers gently over Dad's head. The rain had washed much of the blood away, and I could feel a big lump on the side of his skull, but no dent. I felt his neck, where I thought the pulse should be, and could feel a tiny beating under his skin. Dad stirred at last, and my breath caught like a hook in my throat. He *was* alive!

"Dad?" I watched his face, praying his eyes would open. "Dad? It's me. And King."

His eyelids fluttered, then opened. Immediately, he lifted his head, then groaned. "Sasha. What happened?" He struggled to sit up, and I helped, lifting under his arms, letting the sobs I'd been squashing down inside me finally leak out in little gasps, pretending it was the effort of helping Dad. By the time he'd managed to turn around and lean against the tree, I'd wiped my face clean and swallowed the tears, but I still felt shaky with relief. Dad gingerly touched the side of his head.

"Someone bashed you, probably from behind. You've been out here for ages. Did you see who it was?"

He didn't answer my question. "I came to a couple of times, but I couldn't seem to move, then I passed out again." He was shivering and soaked through from head to foot.

"Can you walk? We need to get you home and warmed up."

"Give me a hand up." Acting as Dad's prop, I helped him to stand, but he wobbled and couldn't seem to focus on where he was. "Is it far?"

"Yes, Dad, pretty far. I don't know if you'll get across the creek." I could hear my voice getting hysterical, but I didn't know what to do. I couldn't carry him, and I wasn't going to leave him here. "Have you got your mobile phone?"

He searched through his pockets and found it. "It's wet, but it should work."

But the reception bars didn't appear, and then a message came up to say there were no networks available. "Shoot," Dad said. He swayed and then half-collapsed on the ground again. He obviously wasn't going anywhere.

King paced down the trail a short distance and came back to me. *We need a plan.*

I thought for a few moments. *We've got two options – you go and I stay, or I go and you stay. If I go, I might be able to get reception on Dad's phone further up the hill.*

Or not. If you go, you'll have to find your way back to your bike and cross the creek. Or find the trail that goes past the waterfall. You might get lost.

I glanced around at the thick bush. Beyond the flashlight beam it was dense and threatening. *You're right. Which way would you go?*

I think I can find the waterfall trail and bring them back that way.

How will you get the police to come with you?

Nicky will help. And I am a police dog, remember? This is my job.

I was glad Dad wasn't in any condition to notice what was going on with King and me, the way we were staring at each other as we mind-talked.

What will I do?

Stay with your dad and try to keep him warm.

How?

You'll work it out. I need to get moving.

Stay in contact with me. I gave him a brief hug. *Be careful.*

You, too. Keep warm.

He was gone in seconds, and I was suddenly bereft and empty. I wanted to call him back, run after him, plead with him to stay. Instead, I gritted my teeth and checked Dad again, testing inside his jacket. It was half-dry inside, but barely warm. No wonder he was shivering so badly. But giving him my jacket wouldn't help; it was soaked now, too. Maybe there was somewhere close by that was more sheltered? It was worth a quick search to check.

The wind gusted and a shower of water splattered down on him, trickling down his neck. I ripped the hat off my head and eased it down over his, careful of his wound. The wind bit into my scalp like icy teeth, but I knew Dad needed the hat a lot more than I did. When he murmured, "You take it …" I ignored him.

"Back in a minute, Dad." He nodded slowly, but his eyes were half-shut.

Before I set off, I called King. *Where are you?*

Not sure. But heading downwards.

I'm going up further to look for shelter.

Roger.

As I slogged up the steep trail, I wished for a cave, or at least a hollow under some rocks or fallen trees. Was it too much to hope for? It was a miracle I'd found Dad. Now I was pushing my luck. But within a couple of minutes I found a clearing and a pile of bedraggled Army-green plastic tents and some empty plant pots lying on the ground. I'd found the marijuana farm!

So this is where they'd been. But had they attacked Dad? No time to wonder now. If nothing else, the plastic would be waterproof. I tugged at the sheeting and pried the pegs out of the dirt. If they'd used it like a hothouse to keep the marijuana warm and growing in this weather, hopefully it would work for us, too. For the first time in ages, the sense of being overwhelmed faded, and a glow of pride took its place. I could do this. I was winning! It re-energized me, and after kicking the pots out of the way, I managed to pull apart a piece the size of a bed sheet and drag it back down the trail. When Dad saw my discovery, he muttered, "Knew they were up here somewhere. Wait'll I get my hands on them."

I wrapped the plastic under and around us both, sitting close to him so I could help to warm him up. I felt like a side of beef in plastic at the supermarket. Being right next to Dad made me realize how hard he was shivering, and his teeth chattered every now and then, too. I snuggled in closer, hoping King was well on the way.

I think I'm near the waterfall.

Good.

I turned the flashlight off to save the batteries, and the darkness rushed in like black water. Dad was drifting off again, and I knew I needed to keep him awake. "Dad, I don't think it was the growers who thumped you."

"Wh-why not? Who else w-would it be?"

"Who tipped you off where they were?"

"D-don't know. Anonymous call. Said I had to h-hurry or I'd miss them."

"Why didn't you call for backup?"

"Tried. Radio dead. Phone no g-good. Then I saw one of them, making a r-run for it. I chased him."

"The person who hit you came from behind. How did the growers know you were coming and get around behind you?"

He was silent for a few moments, his eyes closed again, and I nudged him anxiously. "It's all right, I w-was thinking," he said. "Th-that's a g-good point."

"Was the person you saw a decoy?"

He grunted. "Could've been."

"I think you were set up."

"Who b-by?"

"Whoever is stealing the paintings." This was where Dad would want evidence again, and my head was so cold now that I wasn't sure I could think properly, but I was determined to keep him talking and alert.

"No, it must've been the marijuana growers."

"It's because you questioned Mr. Jones-Sutton. He told someone you were on to them, and they decided to get rid of you. Maybe Connor Jacobson is behind it all." I was sure it all fitted together somehow, but I was missing some connections. Or maybe some information, things we hadn't discovered yet. Oh, for a warm, dry place to think in!

He shook his head, which must've hurt because he groaned and took a few deep breaths before answering. "I can't see it, Sasha. They'd know I'd report what I suspected to the detectives."

"But you didn't, did you? You didn't have time because the tip about the drugs came in. OK, someone anonymous might've called you. But the painting thieves – they set you up and followed you and, bang, you were out of action, maybe forever."

"I would normally call in for backup, though. They were taking a big risk that more police weren't right behind me."

I hesitated. Was Dad right? Was I making assumptions? Was I thinking I *knew* stuff, and I was way off base? "It takes twenty minutes to get here from Marberry. Even if you'd waited at the end of Gold Diggers Lane for backup, they still could've gotten rid of you and dragged you into the bush out of sight." Another thought flashed though my mind. "I bet if you get the radio checked, you'll find it's been deliberately damaged."

"Maybe. I should've checked it before I left base. Stupid

of me. I dunno – I'm used to taking charge. This job's a bit different." He was warming up and had stopped shivering. His brain was working again, too. "How did you know where to find me?"

I saw you. "I knew something was wrong when you didn't come home. King helped me." That was pretty close to the truth.

"So where is the mighty King?"

"Gone to get help, of course. Like Lassie." I grinned – King would hate that comparison. Had he heard me?

But when I listened for a couple of seconds, I couldn't hear him at all. Not even a faint echo. *King!* Nothing. Was he too far away? Or had something happened to him? Surely he was close to home by now. Doubt shifted inside me, tried to elbow its way up. No, King had said to have faith. That meant in him, too. But if we had to stay out here all night …

Stop. I needed to keep Dad talking. "I made Nicky stay home and be the call center, so I hope he understands King and does what he's told."

"I can just see King herding Nicky to the phone." He laid his head back against the tree, wincing, closing his eyes. "But we'll still have to wait for Pollock and the boys to come from Marberry."

"No, they're already here, up the hill, looking for you. If Nicky gets hold of Sergeant Pollock on his mobile, it won't take long."

I hope. *Where are you?*

But there was still no response from King. My throat tightened. I hadn't realized how much I'd grown used to his presence, his quiet, low voice. *Come back!* I was glad he couldn't hear me. I was supposed to be holding up my end here, being brave, helping Dad. I just wished I didn't feel so isolated and alone. Something huge swooped past us, wings almost touching my face, and I twisted back in fright. "Owl," Dad said. "After prey, not us." I shuddered, imagining claws raking across my face, then cuddled in closer to Dad.

The middle of me was warmer now, but my legs and feet were like blocks of ice. I wished whoever was coming would hurry up. The wind was getting stronger, icy drops showered down from the canopy, and rain wouldn't be far behind. Dad's head was drooping forward again, and panic jangled in my stomach.

"So, Dad," I said loudly, "how are you liking Manna Creek?"

His head jerked up, and he blinked. "Good. I thought it was going to be quiet, but ... how about you?"

"I dunno. What's a manna anyway?"

"A kind of gum tree. A lot of people call manna gums ghost gums."

I shuddered. "Great."

"Do you hate the place, or is that my imagination?"

"Well, it's hard, that's all. I've got no friends, and the kids I've met so far are horrible."

"Like who?"

"Mark Wallace."

Dad chuckled. "Oh, golly, if you're basing Manna Creek on Mark Wallace, you might as well pack up and go now. Seriously, though, do you think you might grow to like it a bit more?"

How honest did I want to be? "Maybe. I'm not looking forward to school. At all."

"You'll be fine. There are a lot of good people around here." He hesitated. "If you really hate it, you could always go and stay with your mother."

"What? Her? Not in a million years!" The plastic around me crackled with my indignation. I couldn't believe he'd even suggested it. "I don't even know where she is."

"Burleigh Heads. I have her phone number, if you ever want it."

"No, thank you," I snapped. Talk to Mum? I'd rather choke.

We sat in awkward silence for a few seconds, then Dad said, "We need to talk about this, Sash. You know, your anger at your mum is what got you into trouble in Melbourne."

I opened my mouth to deny it, but instead, the shame I'd felt standing in the courtroom burned through me again. It was worse than my rage because it was all about me and how stupid I'd been. I hated understanding myself like that, thinking I was paying Mum back, and all the time I was just being a total idiot.

"You've every right to feel angry," Dad said gently. "But it's only hurting you, not her."

"That's because she doesn't care!" I blinked hard. I would *not* cry.

"I think she does. In her own way."

"Oh, please, don't make excuses for her, Dad." One tear sneaked out, which made me angrier. "I don't care about me, but she's never bothered to call Nicky, not once."

Dad cleared his throat, said, "Well ..."

"Well, what?"

"She has called him a few times. He didn't want to tell you. He wanted to be on your side."

"My side? What's that supposed to mean?" But I knew what it meant. My tantrums about Mum had forced him to hide her calls from me. Nicky hated secrets like that. He liked people to be honest with him. My anger deflated like a hot air balloon with no gas flame under it. "Oh."

"We'll work it out – don't worry. As s-soon as we get home, we'll t-talk about it, all right?"

It wasn't all right. I hated myself all over again. I wanted to throw the plastic off and run away into the bush, fall down a deep hole and disappear forever. But I couldn't because beside me, I could feel Dad had started to shiver again.

Chapter Sixteen

I didn't know what else to do to keep Dad warm. I tried to snuggle in closer, wrap the plastic tighter, but he'd closed his eyes again, his head lolling to one side. Sick dread crept through me. *Dad, come on. Stay awake. Get mad at me. Yell at me. Do something!*

And then, I heard King. *We're coming. Are you OK?*

King! The surge of relief was like a starburst. Tears filled my eyes, and I was through being tough. I let them slide down my face. *Yes, I'm fine. Dad needs help though.*

On the way. Faint shouts came from below us.

"They're coming, Dad. King's brought help." I wanted to tell him right then about how King and I could talk to each other, but I held back. Not now.

Dad mumbled something I didn't understand. "What? What did you say?" But he was out of it, and the fear was threatening to paralyze me again. I had to move, had to help King find us again.

I unwrapped the plastic from around me and stood up; my hips felt like they'd rusted in one position, taking forever to unbend and work properly, and my sore knee ached. *Dad's in a bad way. Please hurry. Do you know where we are?*

Of course I do.

A few moments later I could see their flashlight beams flickering between the trees, and then they were right in front of us.

"You don't look so good, Dennis," Sergeant Pollock said, bending to check Dad's head. "We might have to get the paramedics in."

"I'll be OK," Dad said. "Help me up. I just need a shoulder to lean on and a nice slow pace."

King brushed past the policemen and came to me. I stroked his ears and then crouched down to hug him, burying my face in his damp fur. *Thanks.*

Are you cold?

Not too bad. The plastic worked really well.

"Are you all right to walk out, Sasha?" Sergeant Pollock asked. "It's a long way."

It was the last thing I wanted to do, but now was not the time to give up. "I'll be fine. I've got King to hold onto."

"He's a good dog," one of the other policemen said. "Led us straight here without stopping."

When you pee every so often along the trail, it's easy to find the right way back.

I giggled, and they all looked at me with puzzled faces. "He's a great dog," I said. And left it at that.

The walk back to Manna Creek seemed endless, and then the rain started again; freezing drops blew into my face and dribbled down my neck. My knee throbbed, and I wanted to give up and lie down, but ahead of me, Dad was being half-carried, and I couldn't stop and hold everyone up. He urgently needed help. Finally we came out at the end of the trail – an ambulance was waiting for Dad, and the ambulance guy said, "Not you again," when he saw me.

I grinned. "No, not me. It's Dad's turn." They still wrapped me in two blankets and someone produced a cup of hot tea. I would rather have had hot chocolate! But the tea warmed me up, almost as much as watching Dad did. He joked with the ambulance guys about his family taking up all their time, and everyone laughed, even me.

They let Dad climb into the ambulance by himself, but then they made him lie down. When I saw him on the stretcher, the ambulance guy leaning over, taking care of him, the rush of thankfulness was like stepping under a hot shower. King licked my hand – he felt it, too.

"Do you want to go with him?" Sergeant Pollock asked.

"I have to go home – Nicky's on his own."

"Of course. How about we go and pick him up, and one of us will drive you to the hospital?"

That sounded like a great idea, and it meant I could change into dry, warm clothes at last. At our house, Nicky was at the family room window, watching and waiting, his face ghostly behind the glass. He smiled and waved at me and ran to open the front door. "Where have you been? Where's Dad? Is he OK?"

"He got hit on the head, so they took him to the hospital. He's going to be fine, thanks to you."

He beamed, and bounced up and down excitedly. "You took ages, and then King came back on his own. I was freaking out!"

"But you guessed what King wanted – that you had to call Sergeant Pollock. That was really clever of you." I was so proud of him – he was brave, too. I gave him a hug and a big kiss.

"Yuck." He wiped his face. "You're all wet."

"I'm frozen solid, too. But you and I are going to see Dad as soon as I get changed."

"Take your time, love," said the policeman behind me. "I could use some hot coffee, Nicky, if you show me where the kettle is."

"I'll make it." Nicky raced off to the kitchen.

I grabbed the opportunity to have a hot shower before I found some thick, dry clothes. I felt like I'd never be truly warm again, but gradually my blood started to circulate, and my fingers and toes buzzed with pins and needles. The drab house seemed warm and cozy now, and I resolved to buy those curtains from Tangine's shop – that would really make the room mine.

I found an old towel and rubbed King's fur to dry it, then sponged the mud off his paws and legs. He rumbled a *Thanks* and sounded as exhausted as me. I ate a sandwich and drank some hot chocolate, and my body sank slowly into a worn-out droop. King stretched out in front of the heater, and every now and then I heard him sigh. I could've climbed into bed right then and slept for a whole day, but it wasn't enough that I'd seen Dad leave in the ambulance. I kept thinking he might've had a relapse, and then my stomach would jump around. It was after midnight, but I needed to make sure he really was going to be all right before I'd be happy. We climbed into the police car and set off for the hospital. On the way, the ambulance passed us, lights flashing.

"Busy night," said the policeman.

"I wonder who it is," Nicky said.

I frowned. Maybe Mark Wallace's dad had been hurt in the bush too, trying to carry his crop out. Except ... I'd seen his van in town, hadn't I?

We found out who it was when we arrived near the *Emergency* entrance. The ambulance men were wheeling Mr. Grimshaw in on a gurney.

Nicky ran over to him. "Mr. Grimshaw, what happened?"

The old man couldn't answer with the oxygen mask over his mouth. He blinked at Nicky and wiggled his fingers. "He fell down the steps," one of the men said. "Lucky he didn't break any bones."

"I'll come and visit you later," Nicky said. "Our dad is in here, too."

Mr. Grimshaw's eyebrows twitched a reply, and then they took him inside.

"I hope he's all right," Nicky said. "There's only him in his house, you know."

"Mmm." I wasn't that keen to know anything more about Mr. Grimshaw, or talk to him either. Everything that'd happened had helped to keep Albert out of my head. The last thing I needed was to be haunted again.

I wanted to concentrate on Dad and make sure he wasn't badly hurt and help find out who'd ambushed him. We were allowed to see him for a few seconds before he was taken off for X-rays. Then we were told to sit in the waiting room, on orange vinyl chairs, but I still managed to sleep. I woke up with dribble on my chin and a dry mouth. When we were finally allowed to go into his room a couple of hours later, his head was all bandaged up, and he had an IV in his arm. I grabbed his hand and marveled at how warm and alive it felt.

"You look just like Sasha did when she hit her head," Nicky said.

"We must all be accident-prone," Dad said. "My head's harder than Sasha's though." He waved at the policeman by the door. "Come in, Scott. These are my two kids, Sasha and Nicky."

"G'day," Scott said. "I have to ask you about what happened, Dennis, and Sasha, too."

"Right. Nicky, can you go and organize us all a cup of tea, please? Ask the night nurse – she's a good sort."

"All right." Nicky dragged his feet – he knew he was being gotten rid of, but he went anyway.

Dad told his story first, although he couldn't remember much. "I saw a man running up the trail, and he was carrying a garbage bag. I chased him – stupid, I know, but I was pretty sure it wasn't the Wallace bloke, and I wanted to find out what was going on."

"You must've chased him a long way," Scott said.

"Not that far. Just past the creek. Then I got whacked from behind, I think."

"But King and I found you a long way up, near the plastic tents," I said, puzzled.

Dad shrugged. "They must've carried me there to make it look like Wallace had done it."

"There were gouges in the trail," I said. "Like they'd dragged you some of the way." That was something I didn't want to imagine.

I had to explain how I'd worked out where Dad was, but I blamed most of it on King. "He was pretty good at picking up scents, even in the rain." Then I added, "Dad, you need to tell him about Mr. Jones-Sutton, too."

"There's no evidence," Dad said. "We can't prove the stolen paintings have anything to do with me getting attacked."

I clenched my hands and tried to keep my voice calm. "You know he's involved. You were set up, and it only happened because of what you said to that man."

Scott looked from me to Dad and back again. "Sounds like you need Garry from CID for this, if it's to do with the art thefts."

"It is," I said, ignoring Dad's frown. "I know the gallery man's part of it, and so is his brother. And Dad, you agreed with me when we were stuck out in the bush."

Dad sighed, but when Garry came in half an hour later, Dad had made up his mind to talk it through, at least, and see what CID thought about it. After he'd finished, he said, "I told you there was no evidence, but we might as well lay it all out and see where it leads."

"No harm in that," Garry said. "We've got Sutton-Jones's Melbourne gallery address in the file. I'll get someone down there to call around and see if the brother is there or not." He left, sidestepping a nurse who came in to check on Dad. Then the doctor arrived and wanted to discuss his X-rays, so Dad sent me and Nicky to get ourselves a drink and something to eat. When we came back, Dad was alone again, a frown on his face.

"What's the matter?" I asked.

"I've got to stay in another twenty-four hours," he said. "That means –"

Garry's sharp knock on the door made us all jump. "You were right on the money after all, Dennis. Melbourne just called me back. Arnold Sutton-Jones was at the gallery, around the back, unloading paintings. For some strange reason, he made a run for it, left the car wide open. They caught him a couple of streets away and then searched his car. One of the paintings still in the back was the Nolan missing from Gwen Alsopp's house."

"Did they arrest him?" I asked.

"Well, he tried to say the paintings belonged to his brother, but they've got him at the station for questioning." Garry grinned. "The game was up once they saw the Nolan – it'd been sent out to all the stations in an email as part of the murder investigation. A pretty distinctive painting, with that Ned Kelly helmet in it. Just the kind of painting a copper would remember."

I couldn't help it – I jumped up and down like a little kid. "Yes! We got them. Isn't that fantastic, Dad?"

"Sure is."

"It's not that simple," Garry said. "The guy's claiming that his brother bought the paintings and has receipts for them. We could get them for receiving stolen property, but that's a long way from arson and murder. If they don't give up their contacts, or who did the actual thefts, we're no closer to solving who set fire to Gwen Alsopp's house."

"Oh." That deflated me like a pin in a balloon.

"Don't worry," Garry said cheerfully. "Now that we've got a lead like this, it could all unravel without too much trouble. I reckon the attack on your dad and this guy driving back to Melbourne with the paintings is a clear sign they're panicking."

Dad scratched his chin. "What about Connor Jacobson? If he's saying he bought the paintings a month ago, and now they're stolen, and he's lying about the purchase date, doesn't that indicate he's in on it somehow?"

"Yeah, for the insurance," I said. "We – I mean, Dad – found out that his business is going broke."

"Have to tread carefully there," Garry said, "but it seems a fairly good motive, doesn't it? Another piece of information came in yesterday, too. Jacobson's caretaker has a record – several convictions for burglary, one with assault. Oh, and his alibi doesn't hold up. He doesn't have a mother, in the hospital or anywhere else."

My brain clicked over and found the final connections. Ka-zing! "He's the local you were looking for," I burst out. "He'd know who was away. And now he has no alibi for when Mrs. Alsopp was murdered. He must've had something to do with it."

Garry grinned at Dad. "Are you cultivating another copper in the family, Dennis?"

"Hmph, not if I can help it," Dad grumbled.

"Well, I'd better go," Garry said. "Been a long night, and it's not over yet. Melbourne will call me when they've gotten more out of this guy. I'll update you later."

Nicky had listened to all of Garry's words without one interruption. A miracle. Now he said, "You mean Sasha might've helped solve all those crimes?"

I couldn't look at Dad – I knew he'd be frowning – but I couldn't stop a warm glow climbing up to my face. "I didn't really. I was talking to Dad about a few things I'd noticed, that's all." And seen. Would I ever be able to tell Dad the truth about my gift? What if I saw another death or murder, one that I could stop? My stomach lurched in that familiar way, and I shook my head.

"What's wrong, Sash?" Dad asked, keen-eyed as ever.

"Um, nothing really," I mumbled, avoiding Dad's question, but then a niggle made another link in my brain. "I saw Mr. Wallace in town. When I was riding out to find you. His white van drove down that little alley behind Tangine's magic shop. I thought she was away, or sick."

Dad rubbed the side of his face, the IV bouncing up and down. "Now that's one thing that does add up. I was pretty sure Wallace was growing the stuff – that's why I was so keen to catch him out there, bringing the plants in – but I couldn't find out who was selling it."

"Tangine?" Nicky squeaked.

"I did wonder how she made any money out of that shop," I said. "There never seemed to be anybody buying anything."

"I'll be following that up, for sure. But you're going to leave it all to the police now, aren't you, Sasha?" Dad said ominously.

"Yes, Dad." And I was. Now that we'd solved it all.

We talked with Dad a bit longer, then he said we might as well go home. A police car was coming to get us. We said goodbye and walked towards the hospital entrance. I couldn't wait to climb into my bed and sleep all day, warm and cozy under my quilt.

"Hey, there's Mr. Grimshaw," Nicky said. "Let's go and say hello."

"He'll be asleep," I said, pulling him back.

"No, his eyes are open. Come on."

I tried to keep walking, but Nicky grabbed my arm and made me go with him. "Mr. Grimshaw, it's us."

"I can see that," Mr. Grimshaw said. His mouth twitched at Nicky, then he turned his beady eyes on me. "I hear your father was attacked. I'm glad he's all right."

"Um, thanks." I knew that wasn't what he really wanted to say. My skin prickled, and I folded my arms tightly.

"I've had a think about what young Nicky here told me. You saw Albert, didn't you?"

I shrugged.

He waited, watching me.

"I suppose so." Why couldn't Nicky have kept his mouth shut? Now look what was happening.

"What was Albert doing?"

I stared at the window next to Mr. Grimshaw's bed, but all I could see was myself, my pale face reflected like a ghost's in the black pane.

Chapter Seventeen

I hesitated, unable to answer, remembering Albert's pleading eyes, the weight of his pain. How could I lift it? Would telling Mr. Grimshaw help? But now it was the old man's eyes that were pleading, and I couldn't say no. "Um, nothing really. He was tied up – I mean, shackled – to a ring on the wall, and he was lying on the floor. Moaning." I ignored Nicky's gasp.

"He was alive?"

I nodded, biting the inside of my cheek. I couldn't bear to start crying again.

"What did he say? Did he have a message for me?"

I blinked, astounded at Mr. Grimshaw's sudden conviction that I really had seen his great-grandfather. "Why do you believe me?"

His face crumpled like screwed-up paper. "You're my last hope. What else have I got?"

That didn't make me feel better. "He didn't say anything. So I don't know how I can help you."

"Why was he moaning?"

I didn't want to let Albert in, but there he was, like a photo in front of my eyes. "He was all beaten up. His face was swollen and bruised, and I think he was in a lot of pain." I wanted to snatch back the gruesome words, worried I'd upset Mr. Grimshaw, but a strange look passed over his face.

"He wasn't trying to hang himself then?"

"No. I don't think he could've even stood up."

"And you haven't seen him since?"

"No."

"You kids ready to go?" It was Scott, behind me, and I jumped.

"Yes." I glanced at Mr. Grimshaw. "We're getting a ride home. Sorry."

"Do me a favor, will you? Please?" Mr. Grimshaw begged.

"What is it?" But I already knew, and I didn't want to.

"Try again. Ask him what happened, if you can."

I stepped backwards and trod on Scott's foot. "Sorry. I mean, I can't. You don't understand –" The words jammed in my throat. I turned and ran out of the hospital and scrambled into the back of the police car, huddling in the corner.

I couldn't go back in the old cell, I couldn't! What if

Albert was dead? What if I saw him die? It was over a hundred years ago. Why couldn't Mr. Grimshaw let it go? It was one thing to find Dad and another completely different, horrible thing to see someone hurt or dying like Albert. It made me feel so helpless and sad and angry, that I couldn't do anything except look, like being a disgusting ghoul at a car accident.

Nicky climbed in next to me. "Why did you run out like that? Mr. Grimshaw is a nice old guy, and he only wants you to help."

"I don't want to talk about it," I snapped, and turned away, staring out the side window. Nicky sighed and moved to the front seat next to Scott, leaving me alone. That was what I wanted. Peace and quiet.

Close to home, I picked up King's voice in my head.

Are you coming back?

Yes.

What's wrong?

Mr. Grimshaw and his stupid great-grandfather.

Silence from King. I didn't know if this meant he was on my side about Albert or not, and I hardly cared anymore. I was looking forward to climbing into my own bed and sleeping for as long as possible. And that's what I did. I snuggled down, closed my eyes and expected to drop into sleep; I was so exhausted it was like I was floating. But something kept nudging me, inside my head, jerking me awake.

Is that you?

No.

What is it then?

You should know.

I did. It wasn't Mr. Grimshaw's plea for help; it was Albert's. I'd drawn him, I'd blocked him out, but he was still there, calling to me. His need was so strong, and he was so sad – I had to do whatever it was he wanted of me. I had to help him, or he'd never leave me alone.

I got up and dressed again with trembling hands, barely able to do up my jacket zipper, found my flashlight and went to the back door. King, my true friend, my friend of heart and mind, was waiting for me. Tears spilled from my eyes. *Thanks for not thinking I'm a chicken.*

You're the bravest human I know.

Easy for you to say. I smiled at him. *You only know one.*

He nudged my hand with his nose. *You'll be fine.*

I opened the door, glad the rain had stopped. The night air was cold and clear, the hills tinged with dawn light, and in the distance a dog howled.

Lonely.

As I crossed the back lawn, for once the sick, dizzy feeling didn't rise up, and I could walk without worrying about fainting. My flashlight showed the cell doorway, black and menacing, then picked up the stones on the inside wall. I hesitated a yard away, my heartbeat ticking in my ears, fast and jittery. I wanted desperately to run and hide, but it was no longer possible. I had to deal with this now.

211

I stepped over the threshold and angled the flashlight up and down. The cell was empty. I was grateful that King followed me in and stayed close.

All for nothing.

Give it a minute or two.

We stood in the darkness, the silence suffocating, and I closed my eyes. Nearby, keys jangled, and I heard hoarse breathing. The scrape of a boot. I didn't want to open my eyes, but I forced myself. Not to see was worse than seeing.

A heavyset man in a grubby uniform stood next to me, holding a length of material. He'd knotted one end into a loop already, and he leaned forward to tie the other end to an iron ring higher up the wall. He turned towards me, and I gulped, my throat bone dry. It was the sergeant from the old photo – Williams. He bent down over Albert, who was still lying on the floor. He was in a worse condition than before, not moving, and I thought he might be dead, but Williams threw a bucket of water in his face.

I jumped back and banged into the wall. My heart was like a trapped sparrow, fluttering and banging inside my chest. Williams didn't seem to know I was there, but Albert did. He slowly opened his swollen eyelids and stared up at me.

"Where's the mine?" Williams demanded. "Eh? Are yer going to tell me now? Have yer drawn me a map yet? It's yer last chance, you mongrel."

Albert kept his eyes on me. I knew he wanted me to help him, but I couldn't figure out how. This was a hundred years ago, and these two men were ghosts. How could I stop this? How could I possibly save Albert? My legs and arms felt like they were set in concrete; I forced myself to step forward, forced my arms to bend, to stretch, to try to grab and pull.

I reached out to Williams, but I couldn't touch him.

He's not really there.

I'd forgotten King was next to me. *What can I do?*

Nothing.

I screamed at him in my head, *Why am I here then?*

Watch.

Williams bent down and looped the strip around Albert's neck. "Last chance. Or you die." I couldn't breathe, horror choking me like the noose.

Albert stayed silent, and Williams tightened the makeshift rope with a hard jerk. "Fine. Rot, then." Williams turned and left.

No! I lurched forward, trying to untie the rope, but my shaking hands were useless. There was nothing to get hold of. My fingers slid past the knot, and I shuddered at the sensation, like putting my hands into ice. I reared back and fell onto the dirt floor.

"I have to do something," I cried frantically.

Watch.

Albert's eyes were still on me. He smiled faintly and slowly lifted his hand, touching a stone in the wall to his left. His eyes closed, a gasp of air puffed from his lips, and then I knew he was dead.

Tears poured down my face, and I sobbed. What good was I? I hadn't helped at all, and now Albert was dead. It didn't matter that it happened over a hundred years ago – I still believed that I could've done something. Why else had I witnessed his death?

After a few long minutes, I calmed down and wiped my face and blew my nose. I made myself look at Albert's body again – but it was gone! There weren't even any marks on the floor to show he'd been there. No evidence except what I thought I'd witnessed. How was I supposed to tell Mr. Grimshaw *that*?

King sat silently beside me, and I knew it wasn't finished yet. There was something more to do. Something Albert wanted me to do. His pain and sorrow still sat inside me like a lead weight. He'd looked right at me. *He'd seen me.* What was he trying to say?

I let his face come back to me, those last few seconds of his life. That was it! He'd touched a stone in the wall next to him. A thrill ran through me, and I lifted my head. I had a task now. Which stone? I inspected the wall and found it, jutting out slightly more than the others, but it wouldn't move, jammed in tight. I wasn't going to give in. Albert was depending on me.

Inside the house, I found one of Dad's screwdrivers in a kitchen drawer. After some gouging and poking and levering, the stone began to move, and I was able to pry it out. It fell onto the floor, and I aimed the flashlight beam into the hole.

At the back was a folded piece of paper. My trembling fingers banged against the stone, but gently I pulled the paper out of the hole and unfolded it. Was it the map to Albert's mine? Had Albert left it for his family? But instead of a map, five words were scrawled on the paper. *Williams killed me. Albert Jones.*

Yes, this was it. The fear, the nightmare, the haunting. This was the answer.

It was like molten silver flooding my veins, running along my limbs, spreading brightly in my head. The gift. It wasn't going to be denied or rejected. It was real, it belonged to me – it was part of my soul. Albert had been as real to me as if he was alive right now. I'd seen him, and I'd done what he'd pleaded with me to do. Found his last message to his family. Even if Mr. Grimshaw was the only one who cared, it counted. Like finding Dad counted. Like saving the man from the bus counted.

I stood on shaky legs, and the silver began to fade, but that was OK. I knew now. I knew and understood what it was. What it could be.

What was I supposed to do with Albert's note? Was it admissible evidence? The police wouldn't care.

King shook his head, jingling his collar. *It belongs to Jack Grimshaw. It's what he needs.*

I refolded it and put it in my pocket, my fingers numb with cold. The cell was empty now, completely empty, and I knew I wouldn't see anything in it ever again. I went back into the house and turned the heater up. I was so tired of being frozen.

But tomorrow, I would give the note to Mr. Grimshaw and tell him what finally happened to Albert. It wouldn't do anything to bring Albert back, but it would ease Mr. Grimshaw's mind. His family's belief all these years that Albert didn't commit suicide was justified, and I guessed that would give them peace of mind, if nothing else. And maybe Albert could be re-buried in the part of the cemetery where he belonged, with his family.

I'd give Mr. Grimshaw the picture I'd drawn of Albert, too. He may not want such a grim reminder, but I owed it to him to at least offer.

What about my peace of mind? I sat on the floor with King, my arm around him, gazing at the flickering gas flames. The molten silver was gone now, but I could feel it inside me, like water at the bottom of a deep well, to be drawn up when I needed it.

But was this the start of seeing terrifying events and people all the time? Was my life going to be one horror after another? Maybe the elation I'd felt after finding Albert's letter would have to make up for the nightmarish visions.

Your dad did say this was a small town, and not much happened.

Yeah? I'd hate to see a busy town then.

Things will get better. King licked the side of my face.

Eeuww! I laughed and hugged him. *Not if you're going to*

put dog spit on me, they won't.

Huh! Talk about fussy.

I hugged him again. *You're not going anywhere, are you?*

No, absolutely not. I'll be here for you, I promise.

And with that, I had to be happy.

Acknowledgments

You never know where research might take you – mine started with an article on police dog training several years ago, and led through homicide investigations into sole-person police stations. Like any fiction writer, I've taken a few small liberties, all the same!

My thanks to the following: Victoria Police; Senior Constable Mark Boysen and Klute at the Victoria Police Dog Squad in Attwood, Victoria; Senior Constable Shane Flynn; Senior Constable Roger Barr; Constable Simon Robertson and Ben, New Zealand Police.

– Sherryl Clark